ABOUT T

Ian Cochrane was born in 19... ...up in the village of Cullybackey in County Antrim. He was educated by R.L. Russell, an advocate of progressive education, who encouraged his pupils to create art from their own experience.

Ian began his working life aged 14 in a local linen mill but soon afterwards he began to lose his vision. After adapting to life with limited sight he moved to London in 1959 and, initially, worked as a piano tuner. Over the following years he would hold many jobs, a lift attendant, a civil servant, a drugs counsellor and he taught creative writing. However, after being approached by Faber & Faber, who were interested in his short stories, he became a full-time writer.

Maurice Leitch, Ian's friend and fellow novelist, remembers how distinctive Ian was in the London of the time: "the neat little man in the sailor's cap who made every celebration and occasion so joyous with his sayings, his songs and recitations, and above all his droll, salty take on life."

His first novel, *A Streak of Madness*, was published in 1973 while his second, *Gone in the Head*, was a runner-up in the 1974 Guardian Fiction Prize. His first novels drew on his experiences growing up in Northern Ireland while his final novels portrayed the similarly anarchic life of young men in west London. His last novel, *Slipstream*, was published in 1983.

In 1987 he was brutally beaten up and suffered from his injuries for many years, as well as from increasing blindness. Ian Cochrane died in 2004.

A Streak of Madness

IAN COCHRANE

turnpike books

First published in Great Britain by Allen Lane 1973
This edition published 2022 by Turnpike Books

turnpikebooks@gmail.com

ISBN 9781916254770

Printed and bound in Great Britain by Clays Ltd, Elcograf S.p.A.

To the memory of
Rosey Pool

The hens were drunk – it was Derek. He got some methylated spirit and soaked bread in it and threw it to them. Then when they started to stagger he went round the yard, killing himself laughing.

'It stops them laying,' I say. He says nothing. He can't stop for laughing.

'It's not good for them, and the master might come,' I say. I was sitting pulling a feather to pieces, making lots of little feathers. Master Burney made fishing flies out of feathers. He wouldn't say nothing to Derek, but you would know he didn't like it.

'The master should bring his bed over here and stay,' Derek says when he has dried his eyes and looked up and seen the master coming over the far hill.

'What's he got this time, I wonder,' I say.

'God knows,' Derek says.

'It's making him better anyway,' I say. 'He can talk now.'

'He couldn't do but better than that Jasus fellow,' Derek says.

Ralph had been ill for about three months now. He just got the 'flu and got worse and worse, and thinner too. For the first two months the faith-healer came, but he never did Ralph no good. Da said it was because Ralph had no faith. But he couldn't have faith – just lying there with the sweat running off him, and him not able to ask for a drink of water or look up at you. It looked like he just wanted to lie there

7

and melt away. Then the teacher started to come and bring medicine, and the faith-healer hardly came any more. He said it was no good with other forces working against him – against the will of The Lord Jasus Christ. Whatever the teacher was giving Ralph it was making him better. That's what I say – because it was only one room we had, and we all slept in it, and I slept with Ralph even when he was lying wetting the bed with sweat and not able to talk. But after the teacher had been coming for a few days he was able to talk to me a bit. He asked me if the tadpoles had come out yet. At school the teacher had a big glass case and we brought jam-pots of frog spawn and put it into the tank. It was like little black ball-bearings covered with thick clear jelly, and we would watch them every day getting bigger and bigger, and one day without you even noticing the change you would see them with their fine wrinkly tails wiggling up and down the tank. Then the teacher would send us out to put them into an old dam or pond to give them a chance to grow into frogs.

'Their tails are dropping off now,' I say. 'They will soon have to go back into the dam again.'

'You listen to the master when he's talking about them things,' he says. 'He knows what he's talking about.'

'I know,' I say.

'I want to talk,' he says. And you would think he had to force his breath all the time.

'If you say nothing,' I say, 'I know it's not because you want to say nothing.'

'I want to live and love,' he says. And I feel sorry for him because maybe he thinks he is going to die, and I put my arm around his wet body.

'The master will make you better,' I say. But he doesn't answer, and I can hear him trying to swallow in the dark. It is hard to say whether he is crying or not. I want to hear him crying because I think he has stopped breathing. 'I don't think we'll get that new house in the village,' I say to him every night and he smiles because he knows I am only letting on – because I know that's what he dreads most. The Reverend Marks came to visit us while Ralph was very ill, and he said that we would have to get a new house because it was unhealthy all living in the same room – and Wendy a girl too and us all boys. The Reverend Marks looked at Ma and Ma said, 'You will,' and he took a big deep breath and said, 'Yes, I will.' So I knew we would get one but all the same I say that to Ralph. One night Ralph says the Reverend Marks is on the committee, but I say it makes no difference.

I ran across the field and met the master at the far gate and opened it for him. Although he never made us do anything at school, we wanted to please him. Ma and Da never liked him since he got Ralph into an art school. Ma said he would have been better working his way up in an office. One of the reasons I liked the master was because he was better than Miss Kerr. There were two rooms in the school and Master Burney was the headmaster although he was no good as a teacher – that is as far as the inspector was concerned. He taught the wrong things or didn't teach anything – he read stories and poetry out aloud and he let children read books that only grown-ups should be reading, and older children were reading books that only young children should read. Da said he should cram a few facts in like Miss Kerr. She taught us that Ireland is an island the same shape as a bear; and Holland is flat and full of tulips and windmills, and they had to build a dyke to keep the country from being flooded. Then one day the water started squirting out through the dyke and a little boy came along and stuck his finger in the hole and saved everybody in the country from getting drowned. Another thing we had to learn was that Australia is in the sky – in a way. If you stayed the right way up in this country and then went to

Australia, when you got there your head would be on the earth and your feet would be in the sky. It is full of kangaroos with boxing gloves on, hopping around all over the place throwing boomerangs at each other. In other countries people were burnt black with the sun. If you went there they put you in a pot and cooked you alive. In Ireland we were more civilized: we could kill people with guns. In Miss Kerr's room we had to count beads too, and if you knew all these things and you weren't stupid you passed into the master's end. I never passed in. I was thrown in to get punished. She said I wrote a dirty poem; but I never wrote it, someone gave it to me. She said, 'What's that piece of paper in your hand?' and I said, 'Nothing,' and she said loud, 'What is it?' And then when I saw the way she was getting I said, 'It's a poem,' and she said, 'Perhaps you would like to read it out to the rest of the class.' So I read:

'There was an old woman from Glenwhorrie;
Who needed a piss in a hurry.
She lay on her back and opened her crack,
And a bloke reversed in in a lorry.'

She never gave me time to look up, she had hold of the back of my neck and she sent me flying into Master Burney's room with the piece of paper still in my hand too. When he read it he smiled.

'Did you write this?' he asked me.

'No sir,' I said.

'Well,' he said, 'take a seat and you can try writing a little poem about whatever you like.'

I wrote, 'Miss Kerr has got a face like a bloodshot eye. She eats the skin of her orange every day at lunchtime and then spits it all out on to the desk and if I did that she would write a letter home to Ma. It's like vomiting orange skin and I can't eat when she does that.'

After I wrote that I sat there nearly all day and he didn't

ask me if I had done it. Then when it was nearly time to go home he said,

'Did you get anything done, son?' I took it up to him.

'It's not a poem,' he said, 'but it's good.' He gave me a friendly push with his hand.

'Take it home,' he said, 'and if you have time, write a bit more and let me see it in the morning,' I did more that night and when I took it to him the next morning, he laughed out loud and asked me if he could keep it. I just stayed in his room from then onwards.

'Thanks,' he says now, when I open the gate for him and he puts his head down in that shy way he does.

'He's better the day than he was yesterday,' I say, walking along beside him. It is good walking beside him, because you feel that he likes you and he is strong and understands.

'What makes you think he's better, son?' he asks me.

'Maybe I just said that,' I say. He smiles and then I don't know what to say for a while. He puts one arm round my shoulder.

'You're right, son,' he says, 'he's getting better every day.'

'I reckon it's worrying him in case we have to move out of this part of the countryside,' I say.

'Yes,' the teacher says, 'but you'll get a new house all right. The Reverend Marks will have to see to that – yes sir.' He says slow, and I wonder what he means.

'The old house could be fixed up, but the landlord won't spend the money on it,' I say. 'He wouldn't give us the skin of his fart, Da says.'

Ralph was lying with his eyes open and a slight smile came over his face when he saw the teacher, but he didn't speak. Derek and Wendy came down the room too when the teacher came in. I sat down on the bed beside them, just across from Ralph. The teacher sat down on the edge of Ralph's bed.

Ralph had tan coloured skin and soft hazel eyes. He pushed the blankets down from his shoulders. He was thin now. But his chest was still a little suntanned, because when the sun was shining, every chance he got he was out in it. He loved the open air. He loved the trees, the flowers, the grass. He seemed to love everything on the earth – every living thing.

The teacher opened his bag and brought out a bottle. 'This is pure grape-juice,' he says to Ralph, 'drink as much of it as you can.' Ralph's eyes turned up slow towards the teacher, and he nodded his head.

'That's it,' the teacher says.

'Will he get better?' Wendy says to the teacher. She was sitting with her dress up and her hands dangling between her legs.

'Sure you know he's getting better,' Derek says. He had a scab on his lip from the cold and it had cracked, or he had pulled at it, and there was a fine line of blood round it. Ma looked into the room.

'Pull that dress down, girl,' she says to Wendy. Wendy pulls it down but doesn't look at Ma. She comes right down into the room.

'He'll eat nothing,' she says to the teacher.

'Never mind, Mrs Oliver,' he says, 'let him drink plenty.'

'I bought him a bottle of lemonade and he never touched it yet,' she says.

'If he could take a little fresh vegetable soup every day, it would be good for him,' the teacher says.

'I got him a tin of soup,' Ma says, 'you can't make soup every day, but he never touched that. I say he'll eat it before it eats him.'

'He said fresh vegetables, Ma,' Derek says.

'He said fresh vegetables, Ma,' she mimicks Derek. 'Will

you make it every day?' The teacher looked back down at Ralph and Ma left the room, and Derek made a farting noise after her.

'Right,' the teacher says, 'I've got something for you to drink now.' He reached down into his case on the floor and brought out a tiny bottle of Guinness. Then he reached into his pocket and brought out a bottle-opener.

'Oh,' Wendy says, 'If Ma sees that she'll go mad.'

He empties it into a cup slowly and there is a thick brown foam on it, like the big heaps of brown foam that come down the river at the back of the house when there's a flood on.

He slides his arm gently under Ralph and eases him up a little – enough to let him sip at the Guinness. The foam sticks on Ralph's lips and he licks it, he sips it slow and the teacher holds him forward, talking to him all the time.

'You better hurry up and get better now,' he says, 'I want to see more of those paintings you were doing.' Ralph nods his head a little every now and then, and the teacher goes on: 'I want to take you a few nice walks. There's a lovely walk up by the salmon leaps, that would make a lovely painting. And do you know another place where I think you should try painting, that old mill further up the river at the Craigs, you know the place is coming down soon – they're going to flatten the ground to make it part of the field.'

'You mean they're going to ...' Ralph says suddenly.

'Yes,' the teacher says, 'so I hear.'

'But that's ...' Ralph says.

'Don't try to say too much now,' the teacher says, 'we can talk every day now.'

'I want to paint that place,' Ralph says, 'I love lying watching the jackdaws coming in and out of the holes in the old wall.' The teacher laughs.

'No, Ralph,' he says, 'I was pulling your leg about them

pulling it down. I know you lie there and watch the jack-daws.'

Ralph's face cracks into a wide smile. 'You,' he says.

'He's talking all right now,' Derek says.

'That's a sure sign he's getting better,' Wendy says. The teacher carries on talking about all kinds of things, and Ralph empties the cupful of Guinness.

'Who's that coming home with Da?' Derek says.

'There's somebody's voice I hear,' I say. Wendy slips up while the teacher is still talking and looks through the door.

'It's the faith-healer,' she whispers.

'What's he come back for?' Derek says.

'I heard him say he was just passing,' Wendy says.

Da and Ma and the faith-healer come bursting down into the room. Da threw his arm out at Ralph like he was introducing a famous singer at a concert.

'There he is, you can see he's getting better, so maybe he still has some faith.'

The faith-healer moved closer and the teacher put his finger up to his lips to tell him to be silent, because Ralph's eyes were starting to close. He let him rest back down on the bed and eased his arm out from under him. Da pushed the faith-healer forward as if to spite the teacher. He was carrying a big Bible and his hands were white and his face was a bright red. His eyebrows went straight across the top of his nose and came right down on both sides of his face.

The master gets up and the faith-healer sits down where he was sitting. The master looks down at Ralph's closed eyes and then at the faith-healer.

'Let him be now,' he says. 'Let him have a little sleep.' The healer turns round slow towards the teacher. He turns his head slow – like if he moved it fast it would knock the steady smile off his face. But before he turns that far he sees the Guinness bottle and he turns quick towards Da and the smile *has* been knocked off his face.

'Do you see what your son's drinking?' he says, then he gives a little laugh – like it was only a joke – like he never seen a Guinness bottle at all. 'It can't be. I don't believe it. A responsible school-teacher working against the will of God.'

'I never knowed he touched it,' Da says looking stupid or innocent. 'It's what I never brought into this house.' The healer stood up and shook his head slow – as if he had just seen the teacher shoot God through the heart.

'It's no good me trying any more,' he says. 'God has given us the will to choose between good and evil, and if he chooses the way to destruction, let him – the way of foul drink. Let him eat away his own body,' he shouts. He walked back towards Da and left the teacher still standing looking down at Ralph.

'I am sorry,' the teacher says. 'I respect your beliefs, but I cannot agree with them.' The healer took a sharp step towards the teacher as if he might kill him on the spot. 'Do you deny the word of God?' he shouts. 'Do you deny the gospel?'

'Yes,' the teacher says, Ma's mouth opened wide, as if she was about to see the teacher being struck down dead with a sword of flame. The teacher went on – keeping his face straight all the time but behind you could tell he was laughing.

'I like the writing,' he says. 'I will have to look for that bit, Thou shalt drink no Guinness.' Ma's mouth opened wider, and I didn't think it could. The healer steps back between her and Da.

'This is the man who is teaching our children,' he says.

'I hope you get down on your knees and ask for forgiveness before you rest in your bed tonight – in case you're struck dead in your sleep,' Ma says.

The teacher looked straight at her. 'If I were God, Mrs Oliver, I would make you stay on your knees for a year for what you have done.' Ma's face went redder than I had ever seen it go before and she started to cough.

'What!' Da says. The teacher took up his case and put on his hat.

'Give him plenty to drink,' he says to Da and went out.

'What did he mean?' Derek says when Ma had stopped coughing. Ma didn't answer. She picked up the little Guinness bottle right in front of the healer and took it down and threw it into the river at the back of the house. Da and the healer stood watching her admiringly as if she had just taken a dirty dangerous snake out of the house. The healer went over and knelt beside Ralph and sniffed.

'I am sorry, Mrs Oliver,' he says. 'But I can't do anything for him while he's in a drunken state like this.' Da said that he thought that that would be the case. He thought that in his own mind but he didn't want to say nothing. Ma said she got a funny feeling about the teacher, nobody told her, but she could feel it in her bones that he drank. The healer said she got the warning from above.

At school the next day I wondered all the time whether the teacher would come and see Ralph again or not. I had all my faith in him making Ralph better. He sat at his desk reading most of the time and we all got started on doing our own things. Some of us were painting pictures, some were writing something and some were doing other things. You could do what you liked and you could read what you liked no matter what age you were. The only thing you couldn't do without asking him was to use the printing press. For that you used nice shiny white paper and your hands had to be clean. We printed wood carvings onto that paper. One side of the big press was full of wood carvings that Ralph had done: you couldn't carve on wood blocks unless you were really good. You began by carving on lino and then when you got really good and could do very fine lines with a V gouge then you got onto the wood blocks.

We all got on very well except when the inspector came in. He was a little man with nicotine coloured skin and a thin neck and thin lips too and black shoes that always looked new. In fact he looked all new. We didn't like him, and I always got the feeling he was holding himself back from strangling us. When he came in we always buried our heads in a book, or if we looked up we put a thinking expression on our faces. The master didn't like him either: you could tell that easy. Two or three times the inspector asked to see someone who was marked present, but who wasn't there. They would be away working for the farmers or keeping the rest of the children while their Ma went into the town for the day.

That day there was a knock on the room door. At first we thought it was the inspector, but then we knew it wasn't because he would have walked straight in as soon as he had knocked.

The master put down his book and went to the door. Then we could see it was Jim Wilson's da. Jim was as good as Ralph only he was younger. One side of the press was almost full of his work too. We tried to hear what his da was saying to the master, but it was hard because he had the door closed.

'He's crying,' somebody says, and I could feel my skin creep over my bones.

'So is the teacher,' somebody else says.

'Shut up,' I say. Then the teacher comes in. He is not crying, but his face is odd – like there was a great pressure behind it. He goes over and looks out the window for a bit. Then he calls Rosie Wilson up and tells her to put on her coat and go home. She starts to cry before she has her school-bag closed – she knows there's something wrong. Then he says to her friend Ruby who was trying to comfort her, that she could go home with her. They had both just been enjoying the same book together just before that.

After they left the master sat at the desk, trying to pick up papers, but just putting them down again. We all felt odd and frightened. Then Jack Carson goes up to him and says, 'What's wrong, sir?' The master looks up and almost smiles – a sad smile.

'We know there's something wrong, sir,' Jack Carson says.

'Yes,' the master says, standing up and talking to us all. 'Jim Wilson stayed at home today to help them thresh the corn.' He stopped and ran his tongue round his lips. 'Well he fell into the thresher, and they never got it stopped in time.' He stopped and pulled his clean white handkerchief out of his pocket and blew his nose, and behind his glasses his eyes were wet and he went out of the room. We were all silent and frightened together – like we all loved each other strong and sad then. When he came in again you could tell he had been crying.

'You can all go home now,' he says. And we all started putting our things into our bags silently. The master had already got his coat on. He came over to me.

'I won't be able to come and see Ralph today son,' he says. 'But give him my love.'

'All right, sir,' I say and burst into tears. I can't stop and everybody is walking in water, and my nose is stuffed up and all I can hear is the master saying, 'There, son.' And in the water I can see he is holding his handkerchief for me to blow my nose on.

When I had finished crying the room was empty. He says he would walk home with me because his house wasn't very far from ours anyway.

We didn't have to go to school until after the funeral. Ma

and Da went to the wake because they had never seen inside the Wilson's house. They didn't see Jim Wilson dead, because there was hardly anything of him left and nobody wanted to see it. His sister Rosie was hysterical and they couldn't control her. They said she would never be the same again, because he was always full of life and carrying her on his back and fooling around – and he loved her the most.

Most of the children from school went to the funeral except those who didn't have black ties. I was ready to go and then I began to think of him and blood and maybe half his head missing, and him not him no more – just bad. I wouldn't go even if I was well dressed. And it was hot, and Ma was going and if I didn't go Ma would be there and I would be at home and Ralph was still sick, and I went with Ma to stand at the side of the road and watch it going past. Aunt Mary was at the side of the road too and Ma had almost stopped speaking to her although it wasn't certain that we had got a new house in the village yet, though Ma was certain in her own mind. And the Reverend Marks coming to see Ralph and all.

Aunt Mary was married now, but she had one child before she was married. Although no one had seen him until about three years after she was married, we all knew she had him. But it was hard to tell because she always had half a dozen children hanging onto her. Everybody talked about her going out with the Reverend Marks, and him married already with two children – both looking the same and like him too, with big foreheads and red ears sticking out and eyes so that they had to look down or look up to see you in front of them – like they had to avoid looking through their glasses. They were known as the star-gazers because when they were walking in the right position their eyes were look-ing at the stars. Aunt Mary's first child, the one she had be-fore she was married, the one that was missing for about three years after he was born, he was exactly like that only he was dim-witted. His mouth hung open all the time too, like it had fallen off its hinges. It was hard to say what age he was, and Aunt Mary took him back from school when he wasn't very old and he never got into the master's end: that was odd, because the master said there was something in every child no matter how stupid. But she kept him at home somewhere and not many people had seen him much.

Ma stood down a bit and pretended that she didn't see Aunt Mary and the half-witted boy and the half-dozen children that were hanging onto the hem of her coat.

It was a sad thing the funeral, but to me it wasn't as sad as hearing he was dead. We all stood along the roadside crying and when we saw four men coming round the corner carrying the coffin and it moving slow and heavy with all them flowers on it we cried worse than ever. It was sad seeing the master and Jim Wilson's father carrying the front end of the coffin on their shoulders and two of his best friends from school taking the back: they were crying too and the master looked like he had cried all the crying out of himself. Aunt Mary's dim-witted boy didn't even cry when the coffin came up level to him, so she hit him a thump on the back that nearly sent him flying under the walking folk's feet and she pulled him back like it was his fault. It was the biggest funeral that Ma had ever seen. There were fifty walking folk and twenty-two cars and they carried the coffin all the way to the graveyard in the village. Da was one of the walking folk and he said that he heard that there were thirty cars and Ma said that maybe more cars joined in before they got to the village.

As soon as the funeral was over we had to hurry back to Ralph because we had left Wendy to look after him and she had made a little house out at the back with bed ends and Willie Glee was her husband, so you couldn't get her to stay in the house now. Willie was only nine and he lived two fields away and she loved him.

Ralph was sitting up on the edge of the bed when we got back. Ma nearly had a fit and told him to get back in again, but he said he was feeling okay now and would try and stay up until Derek got back from work. Derek was a carpenter now in a firm outside the village. Ma wanted him to do that because Jesus was a carpenter.

Ralph stayed up a little while every day after that and the master came to see him every day and brought him a little bottle of Guinness. Then they started to go for short walks together and then longer walks. Ralph loved the countryside and never wanted to leave it. But one day the postman came over to our house with a letter from the Council to say that Da was to call and collect a key for one of the new houses.

When Ralph seen the letter he just went outside and sat on a stump of tree for about two or three days. He would just sit there, staring. The first thing Da did was to sell the hens. Ralph says, 'There's no need for that, what harm are they doing, what harm would they do in a new house?' Then Da put the cat in a bag. It was a flour bag.

'What are you up to?' Ralph says.

'It's got to be drowned,' Da says. 'You can't have no animals down there.' It was a big ginger cat with four white paws and it lay on the window-sill all day. One paw got out of the bag and Da pushed it down in and tied the mouth quick. The bag moved like it was alive too, then I seen Ralph's eyes getting wet and I knew he could hold in no more.

'Yer eighteen and you would think you were six or something,' Da says. You could tell by the way Ralph was sitting that his whole inside was crying – right up to his eyes, and his heart was melting too.

'It's okay, Ralph,' I say, then I was nearly crying too. He just got up and ran and threw himself face down on the grass and sobbed just like a baby does. Ma come out.

'What do you think you are? Do you think you are still a baby yet? Your da and I tried hard to get this new house. It's dry, not like here.' Ralph didn't answer and Ma went on and on.

'I could see the point if you were ill the way you were a year ago. But maybe it's an excuse to do nothing since. And Master Burney and you never away from each other since . . .' Da went round the corner and down to the river and threw the cat in, but Ralph said nothing. He was crying silent and he must have cried all day, not eating anything. Ma just kept going on to him. In the evening he came in and didn't say much to Ma and Da. Ma went on.

'You're as much a girl as Wendy is, maybe more. She does damn all to help me.' Wendy was thirteen and when she was six Ma said she would be glad when she got older so that she could take some of the weight off her hands. But it made no difference how old she got, and I reckon it never would. The only reason she didn't want to leave the old house was because she loved Willie Glee.

The next day Da went and got a big TV aerial and had it up on the chimney, before we moved in and before we got the TV too.

Ralph didn't try to talk Ma and Da out of moving into the new house – he said nothing. And when the tractor cart was loaded up with our furniture, we all clung onto the back and Da and Ralph sat up on the front mudguards. Ma was already down in there washing the floor and putting white on the windows. There was only one thing Ralph did do. He refused to load anything onto the tractor and he refused to take anything off.

I still went on to the old school for two months after we moved into the new house and sometimes the master came home with me, because he still wanted to see Ralph.

Things didn't get any better after we moved into the new house: in fact they got worse. Derek couldn't drive a nail in straight yet and his boss said he would be better off just digging foundations. Ma told the neighbours he was an architect. She knew it had something to do with building and he had to wear a good suit to go out of the housing estate to the building site and change there and wear his suit home again.

Ralph refused to work. Ma got him a job in a shoe-shop and the teacher didn't come so much then. But he got the sack after a week. He told the boss to fuck off and the boss told him to go home and not to come back, and Ralph said he would be glad to. And he didn't intend to go back anyway.

Ma didn't have much faith in any of us. But because I was fourteen and had just left school, there might be a chance that I would get somewhere.

Da got to learn more through the TV, that's all. He watched it every night since we moved in.

We all sat around the fire – well I say fire. It was one of those modern stoves that they had put in all the houses, all ninety-six of them.

'You might as well sit in front of a bloody tea-chest,' Da says.

'It's clean,' Ma says.

'Clean my arse,' Da says. 'What's the use of a clean stove that gives us no heat.'

'They say some people up here are taking them out and putting in Devon fireplaces,' Ma says.

'If they pay for them themselves,' Da says. 'And it's costing us enough living here.'

'Maybe when we get this boy earning some money we'll be able to pay off each week for one,' Ma says looking at me.

'When are you going to get a job?' Derek says to me. He

23

thought it was funny the idea that I would have to go to work every day like him. He said when he had a lot of stamps on he would pack it in : he would get as much on the dole. Ma opened the stove doors : the heat was strong, but she sat there with her head to the side, the way she did when she was planning to get onto somebody. When she sat like that it was hard to say whether Da was watching an interesting programme or just avoiding looking at her.

'There's a lot of people up in here has got venetian blinds,' she says. Da says nothing. He looks as if he is concentrating hard on the TV. It was an educational programme that was on, one of those programmes where they ask a question that you can't understand. Da always had his eyes staring at them programmes. He said they made you smart. He never got the questions right. But just as soon as the chap had answered the question, Da moved his lips, as if he was just too late. The man on the TV asked :

'How many different species of birds are there in the world today?'

'A hundred,' Da says.

Then the camera moved to a student who kept blinking his little black eyes. 'Eight thousand,' he says.

'I am sorry,' the man says. 'There are estimated to be six thousand five hundred different species of birds in the world today.' The student put his head down and the camera moved away.

'I see a lot of people up in here have got venetian blinds,' Ma says calmly as if she hadn't said it before. Da looks at her quick. 'Did you hear that,' he says. 'Six thousand five hundred different kinds of birds in the world, it's a big place when you think about it.' Ralph looks up from his comic.

'What?' he says.

'If you got stuck into something that would bring in a bit of money,' Ma says, 'that would be more up your street.' She looks at Wendy. 'You're all the bloody same.'

24

Wendy was only a year younger than me – she was interested in nothing. She couldn't even sew on a button or make a cup of tea. When she came home from school (she went to the school in the village now) – she just curled herself up on the sofa until Ma made her a cup of tea and if Ma made no tea she would just eat a packet of potato crisps.

'She might as well have been a boy, for all the help she is in the house,' Ma says.

One day she came home from school with no knickers on : she went to sleep on the sofa and Ma noticed.

'Get up,' Ma says. 'Get up and wash your knickers.' Wendy got up. She said nothing – she just got an old pair and started washing them.

'The ones you had on,' Ma says. Wendy just looked at Ma. 'I'm going to get married,' she says.

'Talk sense,' Ma says and hits her on the side of the face. Wendy let out a loud scream – not because she was hurt but so that the neighbours could hear her.

'I want to get out of this filthy house and live with Alfie Roberts,' she shouts and goes up into her room and slams the room door so that it shook the whole house.

Ralph paid no attention to Ma – he never did when she got onto him about work. He looked at Da.

'What good does that do you knowing how many different kinds of birds there is in the world?'

'That's nature,' Da says. 'That's the kind of thing you and that master get on about.'

'That's statistics,' Ralph says. 'They're no good for you nor for anybody.'

'You'll not learn much from that comic,' Da says.

'You should learn how the birds live – watch them – see what you can learn from them. I only wish you could have had the same teacher as me, then you would know about life.'

'What do you know about life,' Da says. 'Learning nothing from comics.'

'I would rather learn nothing than have my head stuffed with useless facts that are no good to nobody.' Ralph says and puts his head back to the comic as if to defy Da when he had said his piece, but Da still kept his eyes firm on him. Then after a while he says, 'These boys are smart – look at the tidy way they are dressed – look at their short hair.'

'How can that boy get a job with hair like that? I have seen gypsies with shorter hair,' Ma said, looking to Da for support – but Da couldn't lift his eyes off the TV now.

Ma droned on and on – I knew that it wouldn't be long before she would be on to me, because she had no faith in me ever becoming a good worker. When I was very young I had to work for the farmers, but if there was a way out of it I always found it – like that time a farmer took me into the middle of a big field to drop potatoes for him. I was fed up in the big field: all you could see were hundreds of open drills and boxes of seed potatoes. More than half the field was already planted, but the drills had not yet been closed. He had carried a lot of boxes over from the big stack at the side of the field and placed them here and there up the drills ready for me to start dropping. 'There's enough there for a good day's work and if you have finished before I come back you can go up to the house and my daughter will make you a good tea.'

I knew if I did all the work he set me to do I wouldn't have finished for two or three days. As soon as I realized I was in that big field on my own I started to think about the tea and the daughter. So I just carried all the seed boxes that he had set out for me over to the side of the field and stacked them up with the stacks. That took me about half an hour and when I looked over the field there were no seed boxes left and you couldn't tell whether I had dropped them or not.

The daughter was a fine generous looking girl of about sixteen who wanted to be a nun. I was only twelve then but I loved her – at least that day I loved her. She gave me a nice tea of cheese and pickles and home-made bread that her mother had baked that morning before she and her husband set off to see her sister who was in a loony bin in Belfast, because she wanted to go into the pig-house every morning with no clothes on. Sadie sat watching me eat, telling me all the time how important it was for her to be a nun. I couldn't understand what she was on about – she said, 'There's too much evil in the world and too many children.' I told her that she was wise and she came over and fed me with the custard and plum pudding. I didn't mind her pushing spoonfuls of custard into my mouth.

After a while I had to go out into the byre for a piss – she followed me. There were no cows in the byre and she said she didn't mind coming in when it was empty. I told her there was nobody holding her out. I tried pissing in one of the stalls but she kept looking over my shoulder and nothing would come. 'Can I hold it for you?' she asked. I stood with my hands in my pockets and she held it – but still nothing would come. One of the stalls up in the corner hadn't been used by a cow and there was a lot of hay on the floor. 'Do you want to go up in there?' she asked. 'It's darker.'

'All right,' I said, 'If you want to.' I knew what she was up to, because her and me were together one time before, when I was about five. 'Take off your trousers,' she said, 'then maybe you will be able to pee.'

'Right,' I said. 'If you take off your knickers.' We pretended to be bull and cow until her ma and pa came home. 'Oh my,' she said and crawled fast up into the corner and I fell on my hands and knees.

'What's up?' I said and jumped into the corner almost on top of her again.

27

'It's them, they're back,' she whispered.

'Did they see us?'

'Yes,' she said, 'what . . .' But they were there looking at us. Her da was a big man with a little tuft of red-golden hair sticking out under each side of his cap and a little tuft above each eye. At first his neck was red, then the blood all rushed up into his face. Her ma's face was red in spots and her mouth moved as if she were going to eat her bottom lip off.

'You go away inside dear,' he said and turned her towards the door, but she swung back round again on both heels in a stubborn way.

'You come right in the house now you skor,' her ma said. 'Right now.' Sadie got up and held her knickers behind her back until she got past her ma, then she ran out of the byre.

'Send that dirty scoundrel home,' Sadie's ma said to her husband and looked at me as if I was sour.

'It's no worse than what you two do!' I said and looked at her – like she was sour too.

'You go in the house, woman. And you get your trousers on lad,' the farmer said in a firm voice. She left giving me one big nasty look.

'Did you get that job done I set you to?' he asked.

'Yep,' I said, 'I finished dropping the lot.'

'Ah yer not so bad,' he said. I had put my trousers on back to front and had to take them off again and turn them round.

'Come on,' he said, 'We'll go down and have a look at that field. A couple more days might finish it.'

'It takes no time once you got a box in your hand and your head down – you can go up and down those drills in no time – if you never look to the end of those drills, before you know where you are you are at the end and it's a healthy job. I'll sleep well tonight – but if you just want to pay me now – I'll run away home, because Ma needs the money to pay the bread man,' I said and held out my hand for the money.

'All right son,' he said. 'You deserve it.' He gave me five shillings which was very bad money for the job I should have done. So I asked him if he was sure he wasn't leaving himself short.

It was two or three days after that when he met me along the road. He stopped the car and called me over. 'About that wee job you done for me son,' he says. I went over – thinking maybe that he hadn't noticed that I hadn't dropped a potato.

'About that little job, son,' he says slow and sly. 'I hope you don't think I'm as stupid as I look.'

'No,' I says, 'you wouldn't need to be.'

'I can see there's a good bit of the Olivers in you,' he said. Everybody was telling me that – Olivers are on my da's side of the family and they are well known for their humour.

'Ah well,' he said, 'maybe bluffing will get you as far through this world as brains.'

Da was still concentrating on the TV and Ma was droning on – she had got round to me now. 'There's that boy there, he knows as much now as the first day he went to school. Ignorant brock, but maybe he wasn't slow – he knew as much as an old man before he went to school – but if you are going to be stupid you will be stupid and no teacher will make you no wiser if it's not there in the first place. Now you're fourteen, it's time you had a job, but if you are like half the folk around here you won't do much – God Almighty, what's going to happen to you? – but there's no good in me worrying, you'll do what you like and that's that ...'

I was trying to cup my hands and make a passage from my mouth to my ear, so that when I sung it sounded like it was coming through a loud-speaker. Ma couldn't understand that – she was too busy going on and on. I sounded like a big deep cowboy voice singing. If I went on like that I would get on to the TV. Then what would they say; or I might get my photograph in the *Radio Times*.

'. . . What's he going to do,' Ma was saying.

There were several things I could dream about. After seeing pictures of men in space-ships I wanted to be one of them. I wanted to drive a space-ship over the village and talk to the people below through a loud-speaker. I wanted to be everybody – in short I wanted to be God. When I was younger sometimes I got the feeling that I was a supreme being with more power than any other human in the world. I could shoot my enemies with a ray gun or bring them back to life with a special liquid I had made. I was a dream masturbater – I flew over poor folk's homes with little wings on my feet and arms, dropping pound notes down the chimney. I come o'er the top and fell into reality – trying to work out a sum, or carrying a gallon of paraffin oil through the snow; but not all the things I thought I could do came to a bad end – I was able to cure Mrs Gult's headache.

Ma didn't give me peace to think things out. I was still sitting singing into my ear and suddenly she tugged my hands away.

'What are you going to do?' You're not listening to a word I say, it just goes in one ear and out the other. You might as well talk to the brush. Did you hear what I said? Did you take it in?'

'Yep.'

'You did. God forgive me but you might as well be dead for all the attention they pay you.'

'I did.'

'What di...ay, you're not listening.' She lifted up the
hem of her ...s and cleaned her nose.
'Folk...w houses shouldn't do that,' I said.
'Fo...w houses should work,' she said and gave her
nos...hard blow – just to spite me, but I just started
s...ough my hands again and thinking – to spite
...oughts had gone away from me. School – trees –
...d – Ma – dead – Da – mad – head ... head. I
...rs Gult's headache. I was young then and smart and
...no more faith in me than she has now.
...ve been doing a bit of studying,' I say to Ma once.
...hat'll be the day. There'll be a blue moon in the sky and
one in the ash-pit the day you study,' Ma says. She looks
me up and down – like I had something hidden round me.
'What were you studying,' she asks.
'Medicine,' I says.
'Oh!' she says, pretending to believe me.
'Yep,' I says, 'I have been studying Mrs Gult's head.' Mrs
Gult lived across the field and she was always bothered
with headaches. Da said what she needed was a man. Her
husband had gone to jail for stealing hens : before we found
that out everybody thought he was a Christian, because he
never spoke to anyone or went to football matches.
'All the doctors in the world couldn't cure Mrs Gult, they
can't find out what it is,' Ma says.
'I'll cure her,' I says.
'She told me it was a haemorrhage,' Ma said – not taking
any notice of me.
'I don't care what it is,' I says, 'the stuff I'll get for her
will cure anything, anything that's wrong with your head.'
So with that I get up and got an empty jam-pot from the
shelf and took it out and washed it in the barrel that caught
the rain-water from the roof of our old house.
It was very difficult to make – but all the time I knew
I was doing the right thing. First, I had to melt some polish

and mix it with Brasso and milk, then I am* *filled the*
jam-pot with methylated spirit. I put in some *salts*
and let it heat a bit on the stove giving it a good *salts*
had to do now was to get a couple of those tablets *I I*
got from the doctor, when she broke her arm and c
get no peace for wanting to scratch under the plaste
had saved up three bottles of them, because she said
were the best tablets you could get – she had faith in the
if anybody was ill around our way Ma was first there wit
the tablets. She recommended these tablets sometimes even
if the doctor gave them other ones; they cured everything
but Mrs Gult's head. When Ma was in the bedroom I got the
tablets and powdered them in with the rest of the medicine,
then I put it all in a big cough bottle and shook it well. I
scored out the name of the chemist and where Ma's name
was I wrote: 'Mrs Gult. There was one very important
thing that was already written on the bottle, SHAKE WELL:
if you let it sit any length of time it changed colour and all
the black went to the bottom. So when I was taking it over
to Mrs Gult's house I shook it all the way there.

'Augh sure you're a thoughtful boy,' Mrs Gult said. She
sat on a knitted cushion, that looked almost like it was a
big red rim round her backside. The house was warm and
smelt of cats and red soap; although she lived alone there
was about ten dirty cups and three jammy knives on the
table.

'Did your mother send this over son?' she said when I
reached her the bottle.

'She did,' I said and sat down at the other side of the stove
to watch her take it.

'It's the best thing for curing hembridges there is, Ma
says. It has just been invented.' She looked at me, then at
the bottle. Her hair was jet black except in near the roots
where it was white, her eyelids were the same colour of
white too and her lips were as red as a letterbox.

'This stuff must have come from America – there's nothing to cure me in this country.'

'That's right,' I said, 'you drink it up.' I could see the black settling to the bottom.

'How much do I take?'

'Is your head bad now?' I asked. She put her hand up to her forehead.

'It's splitting, like it's going to split open.'

'Shake it well and drink as much as you can now.' She put the bottle to her mouth and let it go glup – glup – glup down like oil coming out of a barrel. Then the water started coming out of her eyes and she started coughing so loud that I thought she was going to cough her guts right up into her mouth.

'Keep drinking, keep drinking,' I said. For a minute she sat still: her face was red and greasy and her nose was running, the bottle was half down, then she took a dish drying cloth and wiped her nose and her eyes and took another slug that almost finished the bottle.

'Oh!' she said, 'I feel it going right through my head.'

'That's it, it's working, that's it washing that hembridge away,' I told her.

When she finished the bottle her face was red and her eyes were shining.

'You look like a young girl now,' I said.

'And I feel it,' she said in a giggly voice. She looked steady at me for a long time – her eyes looking like the medicine was melting them. Then she fell over almost on top of me and give me a big wet kiss.

'You're a different woman,' I said. 'You're like a young girl.'

'Ya-hoo,' she shouted and got up and did a little jig around the floor – lifting her skirt up above her knees and yooping at the top of her voice. Then she caught my two hands and we both danced – her going ya-hoo and lifting her legs high.

Mrs Gult told Ma that the medicine cured her, but Ma told her that it didn't come from America at all, it was only a hash that I had made up. It didn't matter what Ma told her – she was convinced in her own mind that it came from America and she kept on to Ma to get her another bottle.

I got a thump along the side of the ear with Ma's hand: it wasn't sore – it was too hard to be sore – but it made a ringing noise like the sound of a bell dying away.

'I was singing Ma,' I says.

'You have been droning on and on for half an hour,' Ma says. 'That gets on your nerves.' She was biting her knuckles. 'You'll send me away. They'll have to lock me up. That's what you'll do to me.' When Ma couldn't get you to listen to her, she pulled her hair or bit her knuckles or started to quiver all over – so that we would think she was going mad, and then we had to listen – Da usually stopped watching TV when Ma got like that.

'You might as well go to River Side works for a job,' he says. 'It's better than working for the farmers.'

'He'll not stick it,' Ma says biting her knuckles. 'He'll do something mad and get caught in a machine or get drowned with all that water around.'

River Side was a textile factory built across a river. It was a very unhealthy place to work. Most of the young boys around the countryside got a job in there. They all said that it was until they got something better, but some of them spent all their life there.

'I know Bob Wright,' Da says. 'I'll ask him what the chances are for you to get in. He's well in there you know, in fact he might be getting promotion.'

'Okay Da,' I says. 'If he says there's a job to be done there I'll go and see about it.'

Da was an Orangeman like Bob Wright and what Orangemen would do for each other was no man's business. They could recognize each other by the way they shook each other's hand, but even if you couldn't tell by that you could tell by their names. Da's family and Ma's family too were well up in the Orange order, we all knew that, although it's a big secret and there's no telling what you have to do to become an Orangeman. Da wouldn't even tell Ma and she could get most secrets out of most people. It had something to do with the Bible and not liking Catholics – that's all I know.

Da went to see Bob Wright over the weekend – he must have given him the right handshake because he said there was plenty of work to be done, and if I could go and see Jim Smith on Monday morning he was sure I would get a job.

Derek kept on to me all weekend about getting a job. I would be sitting in front of the stove pressing my feet against the oven door to try and get some heat out of it and Derek would say to Da, 'I don't suppose the fire will be lit in the mornings when John will have to get up for work.'

'Shut up,' I says.

'It's hard pulling out of bed these mornings,' he says to Da, not looking at me, pretending he wasn't saying it to annoy me at all. Da didn't answer him: he was too busy watching TV. At least he was looking in that direction.

'I'll say one thing,' Derek says, 'it's a long day sitting in front of a cold machine all day in a factory.' Derek noticed that Da wasn't listening to him nor was he watching the TV. He went over and screwed the little knob at the bottom, and the MP that was talking started to get fatter and fatter, then his face slid past the screen faster and faster. Then Derek slipped back to his seat and Da was still sitting staring into the corner. All of a sudden he realized there was something wrong.

'Jesus, Derek – could we not get peace to watch something interesting for a change.'

Derek looks at me with a serious face. 'Did I touch it?'

'Not as far as I know,' I say.

'I know bloody well who messed it up. Who always does it.'

'I'll put it right,' I say. I tried and Ma came in. She nearly went mad because she said that I could get electrocuted. Ralph tried and Derek lay back killing himself laughing, because as soon as he touched it the picture split in half and still moved up. Then it started to crack and Ma held her hair and asked God to give her strength. Da and Ralph and me were all turning knobs when there was just a little crack and the screen went black.

'That's done it,' Da says.

'Try moving the plug,' Ralph says.

'Try shitting,' Da says.

'That's what you get for putting it on, on a Sunday,' Ma says. 'Now you know there's a man up above.'

'That's right Ma,' Derek says, making faces behind Ma's back. 'We might all have been struck dead.'

'I wish I seen Sunday over,' Ma says. 'I'll thank the Lord when this day's over.'

She pointed to Derek.

'There's a boy there you would think he was six instead of sixteen, he had as much sense then. God damn, and all that Ralph boy can think about is that teacher. What will I do. I'll thank God when this day's over.'

On Monday morning Ma had me up at the crack of dawn to get ready to go and see Jim Smith. I had to wash behind my ears and polish the heels on my shoes and put on clean underpants and a clean vest – you would think Jim Smith was going to strip me and examine my inside clothes. Ma said it was more important to have clean underclothes than to have Brylcreem on your hair. Da's razor was in the bathroom and I shaved although there were more hairs on a gooseberry than there were on my face. When I dried my face, it felt tight and I thought if I moved my mouth at all the skin would break into splinters. My Sunday suit still had short trousers and I wanted to wear my jeans, but Ma said that I had to wear my Sunday suit, because Jim Smith was a Sunday School teacher. 'It would look better,' she said. I would do anything rather than wear that suit. I would rather not work. I sat down on the sofa with just my vest and pants on. I would rather not put on any more clothes than that suit.

'You can wear your jeans,' Ma said, 'if you wear that badge that you got for attending Sunday School.' I said that I would. It was a little plastic Bible that I got when I was seven for going to Sunday School for six months without missing a day and keeping my eyes closed while they were praying. Ma ironed my jeans until there was an edge on them that could cut your throat – she wouldn't believe me that jeans were not supposed to be ironed.

The first person I met when I got to the factory was a welldressed man. He was walking along the yard with his arms out, looking as if he were about to take off into the air. I stopped, keeping one leg over the bike ready for a quick getaway, if he happened to be a boss, or worse still one of the people who owned the factory. I had heard plenty about them and by what I heard, it was better to stay away from them. They would give you the sack before you started, if they felt like it.

'Do you know where Jim Smith's office might be?' I

asked him. He stood with his arms still sticking out, his face twisted a bit, then he stuck his finger in his arse, scratched his head and jumped about two feet into the air. In a flash I was down the yard and out the gate. He was one of the men who owned the factory all right : during the war he got shell-shocked and took these funny fits of jumping into the air quite often. When Da worked there a long time ago he gave him the sack twice on the same day. In the section where Da worked they had to boil cloth in big vats for a certain length of time. Da had put the cloth into the vat and sat down for a smoke. When he came along you weren't allowed to smoke, so Da hid the fag when he saw him coming, but he saw it.

'Get the bloody hell out of here,' he said to Da – and him with a cigar sticking out of the corner of his mouth. But in the afternoon they sent for him again because only Da knew how long the clothes were in the boiler. Da had the time marked on the side of the vat, but somebody must have changed it for a laugh. When Da took the cloth out it was all stained and he sent Da home for two days this time.

I stood at the gate not knowing whether to go in or just go home again. When he came on further down the yard he saw me and beckoned me to come in. I rode in and stopped the bike in front of him.

'Do you see that, young fellow?' he asks me, pointing to a big green sign-board that said PLEASE DO NOT RIDE YOUR BICYCLE IN THIS YARD IT IS DANGEROUS AND MAY CAUSE AN ACCIDENT.

'I see it now,' I say, 'and I'll know in future.'

'Good,' he says. 'Do you work here?'

'No, I want to . . .'

'Go into that office there.' He pointed. 'See Mr Smith and tell him that I said you could get a start.'

'Thanks,' I say. 'Who shall I say said it?'

'Mr Andrews,' he says and walked off and left me with

his arms out. I thought about going after him and telling him about the things I could do, but I just wheeled the bike down to where it said General Office.

Jim Smith was a big man; either his suit was too large or he had shrunk. He wore wire-rimmed glasses and his nose came into a big red lump like an electric light bulb and there were little black holes in it. When I told him I had come for a job he just passed me over a form and carried on writing. I had no pen so I just sat and looked at it. Looking through it quickly, I couldn't understand it and I was irritated. There was a girl sitting behind a typewriter and I signalled to her that I needed a pen; she pointed to one that was chained to the desk at which I was sitting.

Name – William Oliver.

Other Names – William John Oliver.

Married or single (it said in very small letters with a very small space to write the answer. So I wrote in very small writing.) I am not married.

Age – 14 yesterday.

Names of schools attended – Tullcrawley Public Elementary.

Exams Taken – None.

Have you had any illnesses in the past year – A sore throat.

Full name of father in block letters – William John Oliver.

I got very fed up. 'What's all this about?' I say to Jim Smith. 'Do you want to know where I shit last?' The girl behind the typewriter started giggling. Then she went into a fit of coughing.

'Leave this office,' Jim Smith says. His eyes were wild and he pointed to the desk with his pen and his hand quivered.

'I came for a job, not to tell you everything that doesn't matter,' I say.

'Leave this office at once,' he shouts, and his glasses slid down his nose a bit because he was sweating.

'My Da knows Bob Wright and Bob Wright knows you and he said I could get a job.'

'There's work here for those we choose to work for us and you are not one,' he says and his lips were quivering now and inside his mouth looked black. I stood near the door but I didn't open it.

'Mr Andrews told me to tell you to give me a start,' I say and stood firm.

'Mr Andrews said nothing of the kind, you . . .'

'Ask him,' I say, pointing to the telephone. 'Pick up that thing and ask him.' He looked at me dubiously and slowly picked it up; the girl looked frightened. The 'phone clicked and he says, 'Put me through to Mr Andrews's office, dear.' He looked at me and held the 'phone tight to his ear and pulled all the papers close to him.

There was a thin cutting voice coming through but I couldn't make out what it said. Jim Smith held his hand round the mouthpiece and spoke down into it like one of those spies on TV.

'I have an impertinent young fellow here who tells me that you said he could have a job. Sorry to bother you about this . . .' His nose turned almost black.

'You . . .' The voice at the other end went on a while. Then Jim Smith looked me up and down and said, 'Yes, sir. That's him – yes, all right sir,' and put down the phone looking at me as if I had just poisoned him.

'Fill in what you can of that form,' he says to me, then he looked at the girl. 'Here you help him.' She came with a new form and set it down beside the old one; quickly ran the pen down the new one scoring out here and there and just writing in 'yes' or 'no'. He just glanced at the form when she held it up in front of him.

'You can start on Wednesday morning,' he says, without looking at me. 'Report to Bob Wright at eight o'clock.'

Although Ma didn't know what kind of job I was getting she got me to dress up all the same. In her opinion it was the plastic on my breast that got me the job.

'You might be able to work your way up into the office,' Da says. 'Once you take your coat off you're beat. You look round when you get there you'll see it's them with their coats on that are getting the most money.' I said nothing because I had no faith in anything like that, that Da told me, any more. He didn't like people in good jobs, but he wanted me to get one.

The light was on and although it was hard getting out of a dark warm bed, it was nice to see the kitchen lit up in the early morning. After Da and me had some breakfast and Da lit a cigarette; him and me got onto the bikes and rode as far as the corner with each other. I felt proud when I turned off at the corner to go on my own. Da went straight on to the factory where he worked. The village street was full of people riding to work. Riding in twos and threes and wobbling in and out through each other.

I was thinking what would it have been like if we were still living in the little house in the middle of the country: I would have had to ride about five miles to the factory and it would have been a tough ride – up and down all those hills – that big twisty one going up towards Mrs Sterling's. Mrs Sterling was a very old woman who lived by herself. She had a nice house; outside she had a nice big green iron summer seat.

One Hallowe'en we ventured out as far as her house, to see what devilment we could get up to. We got the big summer seat – it was heavy; we stood it up and eased it against the door. Then we knocked at the door and ran like hell – as if she could have chased us, even if the big seat hadn't fallen on her and broken her leg. What a laugh – we didn't know it was wrong until one of the neighbours told Ma and made us feel really ashamed because, for one thing, Mrs Sterling was a very kind woman and I didn't know that it was her who sent me over all kinds of comics to read when I was ill and had to stay in bed for about three months. Once you get with a crowd and you are happy, you lose respect for everyone and everything.

I could feel my bicycle holding back a bit and I thought something had got round the back wheel, but when I looked round, it was Malcolm Harris holding me back by the saddle. I could see his big red face and big white teeth like gravestones shining at me. He lived at the top end of the village and in the evenings he stood at the door all the time shouting to anyone who went past, 'Yeh man,' or 'Hey what you doing,' in an English accent.

One of the blokes in the village went to England for a few months and when he came back he had a slight English accent. They all said he put it on a bit – but they said that about everybody – even if they had spent most of their life in England. Malcolm Harris acted him all the time only he really exaggerated.

'Hey, what you doing man,' he said to me – that big red friendly face grinning at me all the time.

'A'm going to work man!' I said trying to imitate him.

I told him about going to work in River Side factory. It was the same factory as he worked in, so we rode there together.

'You'll have to be initiated,' he says.

'What's that?' I ask.

'Oh, man,' he says, 'you'll see when you get there.'

'I got to report to Bob Wright,' I says. Bob Wright had

got a job as foreman over the bleach now and he was a hard man to work under.

'He'll kick you up the arse,' Malcolm Harris says, 'if you don't get on with the job.'

'I don't know where I'm going,' I tell him. 'They didn't tell me what job.'

'Oh, you'll be in the bleach all right,' he says. 'They're looking for young boys like you and if you got to report to Bob Wright, where else would you go. I work in part of the bleach myself, but I don't come under Wright.' He says this as if at least he was lucky in that respect.

'Is it going to be very bad?' I ask.

'No man,' he says. 'Don't worry, it's not as bad as a bad marriage.'

When we got up nearer to the factory, bicycles seemed to come round us from all directions. There were hundreds of people. I was a bit frightened now. It was the first time I had ever been in with a big crowd like that, except on the twelfth of July when the Orangemen walked: that frightened me – all the people getting drunk and excited and I had to enjoy it with everyone else and all those people that I didn't know smiling and pushing and smelling of new suits and Brylcreem and drink.

There were two young men riding beside us now and three or four girls close in front – everyone seemed to know each other. The girls had white overalls on under their over-coats and they screamed every time they swerved towards each other. I would have turned back if Malcolm Harris hadn't been with me. I heard myself carrying on a conver-sation with Malcolm – trying to ask sensible questions about the factory, about what happened to the cloth and so forth; but my mind wasn't with my voice, it carried on, on its own. Suddenly we were in the yard; some people walked with their bicycles and others rode on them. I went to get off, but Malcolm says, 'Stay on, you're safe enough, there's none of the big boys around at this hour of the morning.' Every door and window in the building was painted green and through open doors I could see rolls of cloth stacked on trucks.

We rode up along the side of a stone building and then through into an old half-brick and half-stone building. There was no door on it. It just looked as if somebody had blasted a big hole in it.

If I could only get back to my bed. I slept with Ralph and he always lay with his arms round me; sometimes in the middle of the night he tried to kiss me or rub my chest; he said that I did the same when I was asleep. That was true, I remember waking up and I had my hand between his legs, but I thought it was Wendy I was sleeping with and it took me a long time to realize it wasn't – I hadn't slept with Wendy since we moved into the new house. That was partly the reason why we got the new house, because the health inspector from the council said that a girl her age should have a room of her own. It would be nice to be at home now – hearing Ma going on, but not having to listen or go out to work.

The building we were in now had the river running right through the middle of it. We left our bikes against the wall and went through a big double door, where someone had painted in red: 'Fuck you Andrew'.

'This is the bleach,' Malcolm said and waited for my reactions. God, what a place. The floor was all puddle holes, it was tiled with sand-coloured tiles and in some parts there was a white crust of lime or something like that. There were great big machines with big rollers on them – like they had been cut out of the thickest part of a tree. The river ran under these machines. Stayed onto the roof and walls were dozens of crock circles – long strips of wet cloth were threaded through some of them. The cloth was either coming out from one of the machines, or from one

44

of the enormous pots of which I could only see the tops upstairs.

'What's them things?' I ask Malcolm.

'Those wooden ones are what you call vats, man, and those big iron ones are called cears,' he says. 'Fall into one of those and you'll not come out in a hurry. They are about fourteen feet deep.'

'What are they for?' I ask.

'Oh man,' he says. 'That's a good question. They fill them with cloth and put boiling water on them and ammonia and all kinds of chemicals in on top – God knows why. When you know all about that you'll be able to wear a white shirt and have half a dozen pens sticking out of your breast pocket. That kind of information is not for us – we have the weak brains and the strong arms, they have the strong brains and the weak arms.'

We walked up and looked down into the vats. It was early and some of the night-shift workers had not gone home yet. Beside the vats were the big iron cears with big iron weights hanging onto a handle at the top and a little steam hissing out now and then. They were brutal looking things and I didn't like to go to where an old man lay against one of them with his eyes closed.

'There's a thran old bugger,' Malcolm whispers. He picked up an old stiff-looking cloth that was hanging over one of the hot pipes and dipped it into a bucket of cold water. Then he bent down and slipped round behind one of the vats. The old man still kept his eyes closed but he looked stiff. His face was red and although he was old his hair was still yellow. He had a boyish looking hair style and you could see the track his cap had made round it. Suddenly the wet cloth came flying over and hit the top of his wellington boots. He pulled one leg up slowly and then was still again. Malcolm made noises like a bull, coming louder and louder, but still the man didn't waken, then a big spray of water came right across his face. He jumped and wiped his face with his coat-sleeve and opened his eyes.

'What are you doing you young skor?' he says to me. His voice was rough and dry.

'Nothing,' I say. He tried to swallow a few times like a child when it brings up sour milk, then he closed his eyes again and his mouth was still.

'Mm-m-ooo,' the noise was still coming from behind the vat. Then the noise moved round to behind the cear where he lay. Suddenly there was a great hiss of steam that made me jump too; the cloud of steam went away, the old man was up. 'Get away,' he says, 'get away to hell and give me peace.' Then when he was just about to lie down again another big cloud of steam hissed right round him. He straightened a bit, not too sure whether to stand where he was or to move, then he brings out his white handkerchief that is grey now. You can almost hear the dry snot cracking as he pulls it apart and rubs his forehead and the back of his neck and his forehead again. Then he looks at me. 'What the hell's going on? What's it about?'

'Search me,' I says. Malcolm's voice goes on. 'Mm-m-oo.'

'What . . .?' he says.

'Search me,' I says.

The voice came deep and slow. 'It's time all night-shift workers went home.'

'Who's that there?' he says.

Malcolm comes out from behind the vat. 'You silly old fool, sure it was me all the time,' he says.

'I knowed it,' he says. 'Some folk are easy amused.'

'What are you doing here?' Malcolm says. 'Are you feared to go home to your wife?' Malcolm let on to be véry serious. 'Maybe you wait till the other fellow's gone before you get back.'

'The humour of some folk!' he says. They said he was jealous of his wife because she was much younger than him.

'She'll be needing a wee bit younger than yours,' Malcolm said with a straight face.

'Ah shut your mouth and give your arse a chance for a change,' he says, and you could tell he was getting irritated.

'The truth hits hard,' Malcolm says.

'Ah tell you to shut up,' he says and Malcolm could tell that he was taking it a bit too far.

'A'm only pulling your leg man.' Malcolm put his hand on his shoulder and he nodded forgiveness. Malcolm looked over behind me. 'There's the gaffer,' he says.

My heart jumped – I was frightened of gaffers in the factory. I was frightened of Bob Wright and I had never even met him. He came over walking slow and not even looking at us. He went over to a big electric box on the wall and started moving the handle on it slow. Wheels and reels started waving all over the place, going faster and faster as he moved the handle. Then they kept up a steady hum. Malcolm made faces behind the gaffer's back. That made me frightened too. I could feel that I was getting diarrhoea – I could feel the food in my stomach almost falling through me and I pressed my hips in. He came over, his hands behind his back.

'Hallo there. Are you rightly?' he says to us.

'Not bad guv, bearing up under the strain,' Malcolm says. The old man walks away and Bob Wright makes a face behind his back as much as to say God Almighty look at the sketch of that.

'I suppose your man has been asleep all night – money for old rope these night-shift workers get,' he says to Malcolm.

'Them boys could work nowhere else,' Malcolm says. 'They tell me he has been here since he was twelve.'

'Aye,' Bob Wright says. 'They were lucky to get in here then.' He lifts his cap and scratches under it. 'Them were the days of the hiring fair.'

'The good old days,' Malcolm says in a gagging tone.

'Aye,' Bob Wright says. 'That's what they called them.'

'Do you mind them?' Malcolm asks knowing fine well he remembered them.

'Do I mind them?' Bob Wright repeats in a surprised voice. 'I was hired many a time myself. You got thirty shillings for six months' hard work. Aye, and you worked a twenty-four hour day for that money, all you got to eat was potatoes and butter-milk.' His voice went higher. 'Aye and you slept in the barn.' His voice went down into a low, laughing, mocking voice. 'Aye them were the good old days. He turns to walk away. 'Good my arse,' he says, then he looks at me.

'Do you know this fellow?' Malcolm asks him. He looks me up and down. 'Aye,' he says, 'I would know him anywhere. If he's as good a man as his grandfather, he'll be all right.' Then he looks straight at me. 'You're an Oliver, I could tell you anywhere.' He put his head to the side and says to Malcolm. 'Am I not right?'

'You are,' Malcolm says and they both looked at me; I was rolling my tie up to my neck and letting it fall down again.

'Can you give him a job?' Malcolm asks him.

'He'll need to report to the office,' he says.

'Oh that's all right,' Malcolm says, 'he's been there already and was told to report to you.'

'Dammit, that's right, Jim Smith said something about a young fellow starting today. Come and I'll fit you with a pair of wellingtons.'

I followed him. He walked taking long steps and his shoulders moving from side to side. He was wearing wellingtons that came up to his knees.

We went up a long passage, walking through water all the time, then we crossed a small yard and went into a little hut, where there were rows of wellingtons. He lifted down a pair and set them in front of me.

'Try them on for size,' he says. I didn't like taking off my shoes, because there were holes in both my socks; they were Da's socks because Ma had mine in the oven to dry quick and they burnt.

I turned my back to him and slid my feet into them. They were too big, but I said they fitted.

As we were going into the bleach, suddenly the horn blew; it was very loud. We could hear it blowing where we used to live away up in the country. At one time they used to blow it at a quarter to eight, to give people time to rush to work. Da always told us about the old fellow who worked with him and he was always late and when he got into work he talked fast, like talking faster was getting him there earlier, but he was always late Da says and he always got his words arse about face. He said to Da one morning: 'I put my foot in the horn as the trousers blew eight and left the door in bed and Maggie lying wide open.'

The bleach was full of young boys with wellingtons on and older men wore brown overalls too. When the cloth came out of the machine it went out over reels and the boys were standing on the trucks hitting it with their hands, making it fall in circles. Some of the trucks had been built up to about six feet high with wet cloth.

'There,' Bob Wright says. 'That's what I want you to do. Hank this cloth onto one of these trucks.' He pulled out one of the three-wheeled trucks that was against the wall. I pushed although it was empty and easy to pull. He guided it under one of the reels from which the cloth hung down.

'Get up there,' he says, 'and I'll get one of the lads to show you how to do it.' As soon as he looked around, half the boys who had been looking so busy had disappeared.

'You stay there,' he says, as if he were frightened I would

run away and hide too. After about ten minutes he came back, walking behind a big fat boy who had his head down and was kicking at the water on the floor. He looked at me as if it was my fault that Bob Wright had chased him up. He went round and started the machine. There was a constant rhythm and the wet cloth trickled down onto the truck. I tried doing what I saw the rest of the boys doing, but the cloth didn't fall in neat little circles – it fell all over the place. Some of it went onto the floor and when I bent down to pull it up it started running all over my back and head. The boy came running round and jumped up onto the truck. He moved his two hands easily, slapping the wet white curls in nice rows.

He hanked most of the cloth onto the truck, but every now and then he let me up to try a bit. George his right name was, but most people called him Buster. He explained to me how to work the machine. The cloth came sliding out through the rollers and up over a reel and then trickled down into the water. All I had to do was keep an eye on it in case the cloth went into a knot and jammed the rollers. If that happened I had to stop the machine quick or the cloth would tear.

Buster was a nice chap. At first he seemed kind of shy. He didn't like telling me what to do, he pretended that he didn't know much about the job himself and when we had a break he gave me half of his last cigarette.

'What does this mean getting initiated?' I ask him. He went a bit red.

'Don't worry about it,' he says. 'Don't put up a fight and you will be all right.'

'What do they do?' I persist. We were sitting under the platform where the vats were. It was hot and very dirty with all kinds of little drains taking away dirty water.

'They might put grease on it,' he says.

'What for?'

'They do that,' he says and looks down at the thick, white muddy drain.

'Did they do it on you?' I ask. He didn't say anything for a long time. Then he kind of tried to laugh.

'I had knickers on,' he says and he was sweating. It was difficult not to look at him. His head was big. He was looking away from me. His big head made me feel sorry for him and I wanted to tell him that I was stupid and it didn't matter what he said to me.

'What about that?' I say.

'They seen them on me,' he says and looks around ...

'You might just as well forget about it now,' I say.

'It gets into your mind and stays there all day,' he says.

'Some people think some things and some people think other things and one's no wiser than the other most of the time,' I say.

'I liked wearing them,' he says, turning his big head and kind of smiling. His mouth was an O shape.

'What you like is the main thing,' I say.

'It's a bit worse,' he says, looking away from me.

'You should forget about this worrying,' I say. 'Ma worries all the time and she's no happier.'

Then he says, 'Did you ever kiss?'

'Kiss?' I say.

'You see when I get into bed, I say I'll sleep. Then I don't. I put my arms round the pillow and pretend it's somebody and I know it's nobody, but I close my eyes.' He rubs his finger up and down his wellington. It is wet at the toe and he drags the wet up. 'I kiss the pillow, then it's harder to get to sleep so I put another pillow down and lie on it. Then I want to go right through the bed and turn backwards and forwards and no shape. That makes me think I'm going to hell and God is looking at me. But I can't stop and I say to him, "Just this one time," then I finish and He doesn't say anything.'

'He never says nothing as far as I can hear,' I say. 'So I should just forget about Him unless He says something, but I never heard Him.'

'The priest says that I should think about God and if I keep wanting to think about something else I should put my rosary round it,' he says.

'You just never bother telling him any more,' I say. 'Maybe we should get up there to that machine now, or what.'

'Will you cross your heart not to tell anybody what I told you,' he says.

'I'll not tell anybody,' I say. 'God strike me down dead if I do.'

It was when I was on my way back from dinner with Buster that a big gang of boys out of the bleach came round me. Buster stood back. There were two ginger-haired boys. One had darker hair than the other and he was covered in freckles. The other had a very clean skin and he wore a tie and a new-looking sports coat although, like the rest of the boys, he wore wellingtons and jeans that were bleached white in places.

The two ginger boys came over and took my arms and the rest of the boys gathered round. Suddenly I broke loose and almost got through them, but somebody got hold of me from behind; none of them looked angry. I stood and the two ginger boys came over and got hold of my arms again.

'What's this about?' I ask.

'Never mind,' one of the boys says. He looked very casual. He had brown curls hanging over his forehead. He had the thumb of one hand sticking into the pocket of his tight jeans and he smoked a tiny stub of a cigarette. One of the ginger boys twisted my arm up my back and I leant back with my mouth open. He wasn't really hurting me, but I had to let on he was in case he twisted it up further. He let it go a bit loose, then two or three of them got hold of my legs and arms and I was suspended in the air. I wriggled a bit but it wasn't much use. They carried me into the bleach, and I got the fear that they were going to throw me into the cold water of the washers or maybe throw me into a boiling vat. I lay still letting them carry me and letting them loosen their grip. Suddenly I drew my arms and legs up close to my body and then shot them out with a great force. They had let my feet go anyway – I felt my backside touch the wet floor. Someone was still holding onto my arms. I dug my feet into the floor and forced my way back, then there was two or three of us on top of each other on the floor. I tried to get up, but one boy still held onto me, it was one of the ginger boys. He was angry, his mouth twitched.

'Let him go now,' the other boys were saying. They were standing back and I got the feeling that they were on my side. The ginger boy's lips were dry and had hard wrinkles in them. I twisted myself round the floor and got on top of him.

'No dirty stuff,' they were saying to him. I could feel his hands gripping round the top of my legs. I was really frightened in case he would squeeze my balls. I tried to pull his arms away but they wouldn't come, then I started to push his chin further and further back. It was no good him trying to move his head from side to side. I had a strong grip on his jaws. I could feel the ridge of his gums and teeth under his soft skin. God, my heart pounded and I could feel myself going a bit paralysed round the bottom of my stomach, I thought my body was going to burst. He squeezed my balls tight. The boys were telling him to cut out the dirty stuff. I would have given anything for him to let go. Then I could only see black and felt his skin damp now, I could feel myself rolling. I could feel my arms round him tight and me trying to force my chin into his chest. His arms slackened round me a bit and for some reason I let go. I thought it was finished. His knee just thudded hard against my chest and I felt my head, just above my eye, crack. There was a steady snore going through my brain like a noise that was outside and not outside. It was inside but it wasn't a noise.

When I came round I was lying on top of one of the trucks. Buster was holding a wet cloth against the cut above my eye. The ginger boy who I had been fighting with was holding my hand. He put his other hand on my chest and looked into my face and asked me if I was all right. He had a childish frightened look on his face; I tried to press his hand and say, 'Not to worry,' but my lips tugged down at the sides and I cried like a baby, of all the things, I didn't want to cry – I didn't want to hurt anybody any more. I was weak enough then just to live in love and peace. Everybody's faces were sorry and full of tenderness. At the bottom of the truck boys were saying that they better take me to the office. 'No,' I say. I was frightened of getting Ginger into trouble. They called him Ginger.

'That'll teach you not to play dirty, Ginger,' one of the boys says.

'I didn't mean it honest – honest to God I didn't', he says. Then I heard Bob Wright's voice.

'You didn't mean what Ginger?'

'I didn't mean to hurt him,' Ginger says. It was all Ginger could do to keep his voice from breaking – or maybe crying too. I could feel Bob Wright lifting my hair away from the cut, it was a bit stiff with blood.

'It was my fault too,' I say.

'I'm sure one's as bad as the other,' he says and looked at Buster. 'Take him down to the office. They'll put something on it in case he gets dirt in it. And you with him,' he says to the other ginger boy. I sat up and tried to put my feet to the floor; I felt not too bad. Ginger was biting his nails, he came over and put his hand on my shoulder to steady me.

'Maybe I'll not need to go to the office,' I said.

'You go and get back to that machine, Ginger,' Bob Wright said. 'That'll be enough fooling around for one day.'

The other Ginger and Buster wanted to come in when they came down to the office with me, but Bob Wright told them to stay outside.

'You're not right here till there's trouble,' he says. His big bulb nose is like red fat.

'It's not my fault,' I say, but I am frightened all the time in case Ginger gets into trouble, especially with him: his wrists are long and thin and I can see every bone twitching inside his loose skin. He holds my hair back, holding my head back too. I see his face close to mine, he looks like Jasus. The skin hangs loose under his eyes too. I am disgusted with his skin: one part of me wants to catch it in my teeth and pull it off his bones, but when I look at his lips I am frightened because a feeling that I am going to kiss him keeps coming into my mind. Then he goes over and opens a book.

'This will have to be reported,' he says.

'You're not writing nothing about it,' I say.

'It's in case of a claim,' he says.

'I don't care about a claim,' I say. 'It's my head and I want to keep it out of paper.'

'Where did it happen?' he asks as if he couldn't be bothered with me any more – as if he could only hear himself talking and I might as well say nothing, only what went into that book.

'What are you on about?' I say.

'Where did it happen?' he says very slow and clear. 'Did it happen in the dye house, in the yarn-loft or did it happen in the bleach?'

'If anybody wants to know enough – it'll not make it better.'

'Son,' he says. 'Son, son, son.' His nose shivered every time he spoke.

'In the bleach,' I says.

'Good boy,' he says and put it down in the book. 'Now we can get on. What were you doing at the time?'

'Nothing,' I says.

'I see,' he says. 'And shouldn't you have been doing something?'

'I was,' I say.

'You were?'

'Yep.'

He took a great big deep breath. 'And what were you doing?'

'Hanking cloth and the reel spun round and hit me on the head,' I says.

'And at what time was that at?' he asks.

'I could be dead for all you care,' I say. 'I'm just like that book.'

'Son,' he says. 'What time did this occur?'

'There a while ago,' I say; I feel like catching that book and tearing it in two.

'How long ago?' he says in a light voice and sits back like he was enjoying it; he was in no hurry now, even if I did die.

'An hour ago, maybe,' I say.

'Right,' he says and lifted the phone. 'Send Miss Mailey in please,' he says. He must have just been phoning next door because a little fat woman in a white coat came in straight away; she wasn't too fat, comfortable, as Da would say.

'This boy has been trying to crack his skull,' Jim Smith says and gives her a key. She put her hand on my shoulder and led me to a door which I thought was a cupboard at the bottom end of the office, it just said 'private' on it.

There was nothing in the room but a bed with army blankets on it and a small cupboard with a bottle of water and a glass on it beside the bed.

'Just take your wellingtons off love,' the woman says.

'It's my head,' I says. She smiled – her teeth were partly black and I thought she was very nice, she reminded me of my cousin who I was in love with when I was about eight or nine: I called her names and got her to run after me and kiss me. She was about fifteen then and she had little black spots on her teeth too.

'Yes, son, I know,' the woman says. 'But I want you to lie down on this couch a minute.' I took the wellingtons off quick and lay down on the couch and pulled a blanket over my feet before she got time to see the holes in my socks. She opened the cupboard and took out some cotton wool, then she put some spirits on it and dabbed gently at my cut.

'You're a brave boy,' she says, because although it smarted like hell, I didn't scream; I only stiffened my body. She was leaning close to my face, her lips tightened slightly every time she dabbed the wound. Her face was soft and white and her eye-lashes were little curvy lines of stiff black hair. I could feel her breath warm on my face – it smelt a bit nasty, but I thought I could love a woman like that no matter how her breath smelt. I remember someone Da talked about, who said they loved their girl friend so much, they could eat her shit.

'Is this your job?' I asked her.

'Amongst other things,' she says. I felt every time she touched me she wanted to put her arms round me and cuddle me.

'Now we'll have a bit of plaster on this, my love,' she says. I liked that. I wanted her to say, 'My love' again – I almost asked her to. She opened the cupboard and without looking brought out a box of plasters; she got one to fit and put some cream on it and a little bit of cotton wool. Then she smoothed the plaster down at both sides. Her eyes were like shiny blobs of black ink and they seemed to quiver full of life.

'How's that?' she asks.

'It feels all right,' I say. I liked the feeling of the sticking plaster on me.

'My head feels a bit sore,' I say, lying back and searching for a pain. She brought out a little bottle of pills and emptied two into my hand.

'Take those,' she says. 'And then you better have the rest of the day off.'

'I better tell somebody,' I say. 'You see this is my first day.' She gave me a little glass of water to wash the pills down.

'You leave that with me love,' she says. 'You'll get no medal for killing yourself here.'

When I got home and in the back door, the house nearly drove me mad. Ma didn't have time to look at me – to see the plaster above my eye. She was too busy going round and round the mat in front of the fire.

'Jasus, Ma, where in God's name did you get that thing?' She couldn't hear me – she couldn't hear anything – the thing she was holding was sucking at the mat like mad.

'Ma, Ma, Christ a'm home too early!' She tapped a button on top with her foot and it stopped.

'Where did you get that thing?' I ask. She was standing ready to start it again, holding her foot just above the button ready to press, as soon as she heard what I wanted to say.

'It's a Hoover,' she says and pressed the button. The test card was on the TV and there were white crackly lines running through it; she went on Hoovering all over the place, up stairs and all.

We were sitting around waiting for Ma to put on the potatoes for the dinner when Da came in; you could tell it was Da when he came into the scullery, because just after the snap of his bicycle clips coming off he gave a great big sniff.

The Hoover was in the middle of the kitchen – but he said nothing – he didn't even look at it, he went into the hall and hung up his coat, no one knew what he might say. Derek hummed a little tune, as much as to say, 'It's got nothing to do with me' – but watching all the time for the row to start. Da sits down on the sofa and opens his shoes – he still says nothing. Ma doesn't look at the Hoover now either. Derek sings loud – 'Oh there's a hair on this and there's a hair on that and there's a hair on my dog Tiny, but I know a place where there is no hair on the girl I left behind me.' Then he says, 'Brrrr, I am a vacuum cleaner,' but still Da says nothing. Wendy is curled up on the sofa so that Da has to sit on the edge.

'You should go down to the doctor – feeling tired like that all the time,' Da says. Derek gets down on the floor, Ma is standing against the stove saying nothing – Derek gets over on his hands and knees and growls like a dog.

'You're mad,' Ma says.

He lets his head fall and says, very very slowly, 'You think I am mad.' Then he tries to bite Ma's legs; she laughs at first. Then he does bite her and she kicks at him, saying, 'You're not all there.'

'You need your head looking at,' Da says, trying to lie back on the sofa and gets irritated because Wendy is curled up behind him. Derek gets up and comes over and bites at Wendy's ear, he has good teeth and snaps at them – just missing the lobes of her ear.

'Away and sit down,' Da says. 'And give people peace.' Then he sees the plaster on my head. 'What happened to you boy?' he asks.

'He tripped over a straw and a hen kicked him,' Derek says. Nobody laughs. Then he picks up the long tube of the vacuum cleaner and talks into it like the interviewers on TV. 'Believe you are going to fight for the heavyweight title again,' he says and then holds the tube over to me.

'Yes,' I say.

Then he says into the tube, 'Was this a straight knock-out or were you defeated on points?'

'It was a knock-out in the third round, an upper cut,' I says.

Then Derek goes over to Ma and holds the tube up to her. 'I believe Mrs Oliver, that you had a ring-side seat at this fight.'

'For God sake are you as mad as you put on,' Ma says and tries to push the tube away from her mouth.

'You will see viewers, that obviously Mrs Oliver is somewhat distressed about her son's injuries. Now we go over to his trainer, who has been behind this lad all the way.' He goes over to Da. 'I believe, sir, that this young man has been in strict training since July.'

'Jasus, you are a fool Gormical,' Da says and tries not to laugh.

'Obviously his trainer is disappointed and distressed,' Derek says.

'Is the dinner ready?' Da says to Ma. She was standing with her back to the stove like she had just been waiting for Da to ask that question.

'I'm just going to put the potatoes on now,' she says. 'I have never been off my feet all day.' She goes into the scullery and brings out a big pot and puts it on the stove. Ralph come down the stairs.

'Is the dinner ready?' he asks.

'I have only got two hands you know,' Ma says. Ralph lifts the lid of the pot.

'The water's not even boiling,' he says. He is annoyed but he tries not to show it, as if he doesn't care.

'I'll just have a bit of bread and cheese,' he says, and sits down to read the paper.

'What were you doing up the stairs all this time?' Ma asks.

60

'I was on the toilet,' he says. Ma looks at the clock.

'It doesn't take you all that time.' He doesn't say anything.

'What do you get to do up there for half-an-hour?' Ma asks him.

'Did you flush it?' Da asks.

'Mmmm,' Ralph says and still reads the paper.

'He was sitting on there, reading the paper,' Ma says. 'He would need a bathroom to himself.'

'Somebody doesn't flush it,' Da says.

'Somebody does it all over the side,' Ma says. 'I would be ashamed to let anybody up in there.'

'If you got toilet paper instead of newspaper,' Ralph says. 'Then it would go down the hole.'

'You must eat the bloody toilet paper,' Ma says. 'I put a new roll up there yesterday.'

'By the sound of Ralph sometimes I think he does most of it in his trousers,' Derek says.

'If you had to wash his drawers you would know that,' Ma says. She got on to Ralph all the time for farting loud: when we were in the old house in the country it was all right, but now he let them go, even when the front door was open and even if somebody was at the front door selling Bibles or something.

'He would fart in front of the Queen,' Ma says.

'I suppose you think she doesn't fart,' Ralph says. 'Maybe you think her farts smell of perfume.'

Wendy looks up from behind Da. 'Can't you talk about something else for a change,' she says.

'Go back to sleep,' Derek says.

'Better farting than wasting money on vacuum cleaners,' Ralph says to Ma.

'Oh-oh-oh,' Derek says. 'That was well put in.'

Da looks at the vacuum cleaner. 'Where did you borrow that?' he asks Ma.

'Borrow, borrow – he says, borrow Ma,' Derek says, trying to get things going.

'Work, work I could work my fingers to the bone and what thanks would I get,' Ma says.

'I could work myself to an early grave.' She stopped a minute. 'Maybe that's what you want?' she looked at Da.

'Them boys can come round and sell you anything,' he says. 'Even if you have no carpet.'

'It's all right for them out at work all day. They can't see what's to be done in the house. They finish at six o'clock and that's the end. But I'm on my feet from when I get up in the morning till I go to bed at night and not a one would lift a finger to help me. There's a girl there, she has been lying there like an old woman since she came in, and people say to me, you're lucky, you got a girl to help you. Little do they know she wouldn't get up from her lazy arse if the house was falling down round her. I don't tell the neighbours that a girl of fourteen wouldn't dry a cup. I'm ashamed, but you'll not always have me to run after you to pick things up you throw at your arse; then you ask me what I got that for.'

'Maybe that'll do,' Da says. 'Maybe that's a long enough sermon before we eat.'

'Where are you going to get the money from to pay for it?' Ralph says.

'You can be sure it'll not come out of your pocket,' Ma says. 'Because you're earning damn all. All you think about it that teacher and art or some fool thing, you can be sure he'll put nothing in your pocket.'

'That's no reason to waste money,' he says. 'Just because I got a job we're no millionaires, I say there's no need to spend it before I get it.'

'God almighty,' Ma says. 'Are you all on to me. What have I done on ye.' She holds both hands against her face and thumps the ground with one foot. Then she is crying and I don't know what to do.

'I'm only saying you shouldn't waste money,' Ralph says, but she can't hear him for crying.

'All right,' Da says to Ralph. 'You got her upset, now are you happy?'

'Well I was only saying . . .'

'Shut up about it now,' I say.

Too much fuss was bad for Ma. Since she come to the village she went in for tablets and the doctor had to give her blue ones to keep her from getting worked up. They didn't work all that well because she was highly strung. He had to give her yellow ones too and they didn't work but she had more faith in them.

'You all shut up,' Wendy says.

'If you would give Ma a hand in the house instead of lying there all the time,' I say.

'Blame me now she's crying. I suppose it's all my fault.'

'It's everybody's fault,' Da says. 'There's always something to complain about.'

'I was only saying you shouldn't waste money,' Ralph said and Ma sobbed harder than ever.

'Shut up.' I shouts.

'If your Ma gets something to make the work easier then what's wrong with that,' Da says. 'You know it's hard work keeping the place clean.'

'I could clean it in five minutes,' Ralph says.

'I never see you doing it,' Derek says.

'You run around there like a bloody old woman,' Da says. 'I never seen a pansy like you, nothing is ever right for you.'

'Everybody shut up now,' I shouts.

'What's for the dinner?' Ralph asks Ma and her still crying. She didn't answer.

'What's for dinner?' he asks again. She throws herself off

the wall and goes upstairs, slamming the door so that it nearly brought the pictures down.

'What is for dinner?' Ralph asks Da.

'How in heaven's name would I know?' he says.

When we look in the larder we find nothing but a bit of butter.

'It would be far better buying something to eat instead of a vacuum cleaner,' Ralph says.

'It's over and done with now,' Da says. 'Forget about it.'

'Ten bob a week for nothing,' Ralph says.

Da mashes the potatoes and we have a plate of that with a lump of butter in the middle.

I was okay the next morning, but I didn't go to work. Ma wakened me early. She had been up early because the milkman knocked at the door to tell her that Aunt Mary was coming to visit us. She didn't know what to do. She had told the neighbours that Aunt Mary was no relation of ours: it just happened that she had the same name and lived near us when we were in the country.

'Maybe they'll not come,' she says, walking in and out of the room all morning until in the end I had to get up.

'Maybe if she does come she'll not bring the children,' she says.

'You mean the boy,' I say.

'It was a fall he got when he was a baby,' Ma says.

'Aunt Mary says she never let him fall,' I say.

'She doesn't remember it,' Ma says. 'The others are all right.'

'It's too soon to tell yet,' I say.

'Well,' Ma says. 'There's no trace of anything like that in our side of the family.'

Ma thought if she pretended to be out it would be okay. But then they might get talking to the neighbours.

Aunt Mary came all right. We saw her from the window, her and half-a-dozen children.

'Them's not all hers,' I say. There's two or three stacked in the pram on top of each other and a couple holding on to her coat-tails.

Ma opens the door quick to let her in before all the neighbours got time to get to their windows. The dim-witted one wasn't there and Ma thought she might be lucky enough not to have him.

'Where's the big boy?' she asks Aunt Mary.

Aunt Mary looks round. 'Oh God,' she says. 'He was behind me a while back.'

'Did you walk all the way?' Ma asks, maybe hoping that Aunt Mary would forget about the dim-witted one.

'We did,' Aunt Mary says. 'And them big farmers flying by in their cars. They wouldn't stop if you had walked your feet off.' She got the pram into the hall and pulled a couple that were standing on the step in too. 'Where did that big goof go to?'

'Maybe he went on down to the shop for an ice-cream,' Ma says.

'Damn the shop,' Aunt Mary says. 'That stupid brock couldn't go for a shit on his own.'

There was a terrible smell of sour babies in the hall now. Aunt Mary had her hair cut into a V at the back like a teddy boy, she wore a brown coat with a big badge of a shamrock stuck in the breast. She pushed all the children into the living-room and then slammed the door quick and went out onto the step. The children all started crying as soon as she slammed the door, as if that's what was expected of them.

'God give me strength,' Ma said, when she heard Aunt Mary's voice shout on the front step. She was shouting for the dim-witted boy. Where she lived in the country you did shout when you wanted the children. Ma did for us, but she never did it since we moved down into the new housing estate.

Aunt Mary was standing on the step like a rooster – shouting her head off.

He came walking up the footpath, not looking at his Ma, but looking at a picture. His head was down and his mouth was open. She went out and hit him on the side of the ear and pushed him and the picture in in front of her. He didn't cry. He didn't look at us. He just looked at the picture. It was damp paper. 'Didn't I tell you not to tear that off?' Aunt Mary said to him.

They had to pass the Faith Mission hall to come to our house and he had pulled the picture off the board outside. It was a picture of Christ on a cross with blood running out of His hands. His feet were still stuck on the board. It said on His chest CHRIST DIED FOR YOU. Aunt Mary snatched it off him and stuck it in the fire. Two of the children held onto her legs as if me or Ma or Ralph were going to eat them.

'These are not all yours?' Ma asks.

'No fear,' she says. 'Two's too many. That's what I say. No they're from across the field. She's going to have another.'

The boy sat on the sofa with his head drooping. He was a big boy with jeans on and a black blazer with silver buttons on it. He had a row of badges up the lapel of his coat. One said ESSO EXTRA on it and another said BP and at the bottom was a gollywog. One of his sleeves was so shiny where he had wiped his nose on it that you could almost use it as a mirror.

They stayed all day. Ma didn't give them much to eat, thinking all the time that they would go. The first wrong thing Ma did was to show the simple boy the bathroom.

'Here, son,' she says. 'That's where you pee, or if you want to sit down.' She was frightened of him doing it on the sofa or something. 'You push that handle down when you have finished, like that,' she says. 'And it all goes away.' She pushed down the handle and the water gushed down into the pot, but a razor blade that someone had thrown in still stayed at the bottom. The simple boy caught on fast: we couldn't get him out of the bathroom. Every time the tank filled up he flushed it again. One of the little girls wanted to flush it too and she stood up on the seat to reach the handle, the seat broke and one of her feet went down into the water.

Ma always went to the bottom of the stairs and shouted for the boy to come down for a biscuit. He always came down, but he didn't eat the biscuit. He went up the stairs again when he got a chance and flushed it down the toilet. Ma didn't know what to do, because she didn't want him to go outside either, she kept making hand signals in the scullery for Ralph to take him up into one of the rooms to show him his paintings.

'He's not wise enough for that,' Ralph says loud and Ma nearly went mad. She thought Aunt Mary might have heard him say that. She nipped Ralph hard on the arm and smiled and says loud and casually: 'Maybe you can teach your cousin to paint. Wouldn't that be nice?'

Then Ralph says, 'What did you nip me for?' and Ma sang. The little girls all went out to the back and filled milk bottles from the drain-pipe and threw water at each other. Then they went to the house next door and blocked the drain-pipe with an old dish-cloth from our shed. The woman next door came and said to Ma that she liked children, but she was frightened in case they tried to drink the soapy water from her drain-pipe. So it would be better if they stayed in our yard, where someone could keep an eye on them.

Aunt Mary said she would love to live in the housing estate and she asked Ma if she knew anybody on the council. Ma said that she didn't and that as far as she knew they were only giving houses to people with no homes at all now. Aunt Mary said that she had put her name on the waiting list anyway. Aunt Mary also told Ma that her husband had got a job in the River Side factory and that if she got into a new house it would be handy for him.

When Derek got home they still hadn't gone. He thought it was a big laugh, the dim-witted boy. Ralph was trying to teach him to paint when Derek came in. The boy stood in the room looking at Ralph mixing the paint. He was looking at Ralph as if he was mad and Ralph looked at him as if he was mad too, but there was a bit of sympathy in Ralph's eyes. The boy was frightened to take the paint brush in his hand and he always kept looking back towards the door. Then he went over and held onto Ralph's hand and wouldn't let go and he put his hand gently over Ralph's lips and stroked them. Ralph's face got sadder looking. I pretended to read a book. Ralph got up from the piece of paper that he was putting the paint on; the boy still held onto his hand and kept touching him with the other hand. He turned round quick. The boy drew his hand back and looked hurt. Ralph went to move away, but he couldn't. He had to put his arm round the boy. The boy put his head against Ralph, like the way a friendly cat would do, his mouth hanging open looking at the one foot all the time. They stood there for a long time. They were silent and the boy seemed to be happy now. Then Ralph put his head down and touched the boy with his lips on the ear and pushed himself free. The boy was going after him when Derek came in. He made an ugly looking face and growled at the boy. The boy didn't seem surprised.

'Pay no attention to him, son,' Ralph says.

'I am going to eat you,' Derek says in a deep voice. The boy looked towards Ralph now.

'Have some sense,' Ralph says. 'You were a big coward yourself at school.'

'Can you speak?' Derek says. The boy just stood. 'Are you a silly bastard? What are you?' The boy puts his hand onto the bed and rubs the bedspread. Then Derek sticks his fingers into the black paint and puts two marks down each side of the boy's face and a spot on his forehead.

'Have some bloody sense,' Ralph says and goes over to the door. The boy followed immediately and tries catching his hand. Ralph holds him back by his blazer and that was the first time I heard him make a noise. It was a terrifying noise and Ralph let go. Derek went downstairs and Ralph went into the bathroom and showed him how to turn on the taps and let him flush the toilet, then when the boy was standing staring at one of the taps running, he went downstairs too.

Downstairs Derek kept lifting the little girls onto his knees. They cried and Ma says, 'That's Derek, he's not happy till he has all the children happy.'

When they were all really frightened of him, as soon as they picked something up, Aunt Mary says, 'If you don't leave that down Derek will take you away,' and Derek reached his hand out towards them and growled.

Aunt Mary had just announced for the seventh time that she must go. She had gathered all the children together and levered little things out of their tight fists, like tubes of lipstick and earrings, and pushed them into coats and piled them into the pram. Suddenly there was a kind of scream upstairs. Ma held her face in her hands and went stiff. Ralph and I ran upstairs. The dim-witted boy was lying in the bath with it overflowing and the taps still running too. One leg was sticking out over the side and the other one was moving up and down like he was swimming. He was lifting his head up and down. You couldn't tell whether he was enjoying it or frightened. Ralph got hold of his legs and I got hold of his shoulders and we dragged him out; we had the bathroom door closed to make room to get him out and Ma was almost breaking the handle off, saying, 'Jasus Christ – God Almighty – Jasus Almighty. Christ above us today.'

When we got the dim-witted boy out, there was water running out of his mouth. Ralph and I just looked at him. He grinned with his mouth still open and flung himself back in. Ma howled like a dog outside when she heard the splash.

'Let him drown,' I says. 'What's the use of it as silly as that.'

'I think it's something in him that makes him do that. Something even he doesn't know about,' Ralph says. We drag him out again. His hair is sticking to him. It is thin and you can see the white skin of his skull. Ralph pulls the plug out of the bath and I open the door. It is hard to open because Ma is pressing hard against it, trying to get in. When she sees the dim-witted boy and the water running out of him, she has a heart attack – she can't stand. It is too much for her senses to take all at once; she leans against the wall and holds her chest with one hand and a wisp of hair with the other. Aunt Mary rushes in. There are too many of us in the bathroom now.

She hits the boy a thump on the back. The water is running out of him.

'I'll kill you. I'll knock the life out of you,' she says. Water is running out of his nose and his mouth is still open. He makes towards the door, but Ma is in the way. Aunt Mary pulls at his blazer, trying to get it off. He doesn't understand what she's trying to do and she hits him again, hard, and his mouth closes and his eyes close and he cries silently. Ralph just hits Aunt Mary on the mouth before he even knows he has done it.

She turns round and swipes at him, and when Ralph jerks back to save himself the bathroom cabinet that Da put up just after we moved in comes off the wall and crashes into the bath: the mirror on the front breaks and the bath cracks. Ma cries, but not an ordinary cry – it's as if she's just working up to go right off her head, as if she can't help herself any more.

'Just leave him,' Ralph says. 'Let him be.' Aunt Mary catches hold of his wrists and pushes at him. 'Calm down now,' he says, trying to talk nice to her, as if he could understand she was upset now, but she would have to take a grip on herself.

'Nobody will tell me how to bring up my children,' she says, still pushing at him. Derek is in the bathroom too now. He is strong. He catches Aunt Mary by the elbows and pushes her out the door, then he tells Ma to pull herself together and catches her hands to take her out too, but she has still lost control over her senses and bites at his hands like an animal and stays against the wall. He gets hold of one hand and squeezes it. Ma shouts. 'Will you come out or will I squeeze harder?' he says. She kicks at him but he gets the other hand and bends it back till Ma has to crouch to make it less painful.

'God damn you,' she says, and still crouching she goes backwards out of the bathroom. We all go out and leave the boy in. All the children are trying to come up the stairs and Aunt Mary puts them all down again. Then she looks up at Ralph.

'Fucking artist,' she says. 'That's what you call yourself.'

Ma opened her mouth as if she had just seen a murder. She tried to be nice. 'We're not in the country now, Mary,' she said. 'You can use language like that at home, but try and keep your voice down when you're here.'

'Who the fuck do you think you are?' Aunt Mary shouts. 'You're only in a council house, you know. You're not in Buckingham Palace.' She opened the door and was pushing the children out in front of her. 'I'll tell you, I'm every bit as good as you,' she shouted up at Ma. Ma had her fingers in her mouth and was biting them. 'I suppose you're ashamed of me now,' Aunt Mary continued. 'But you're just shit, you're nothing. You think you're Lady Muck, don't you? But I'm clean inside.' Ma ran into one of the rooms and slammed the door, but that didn't stop Aunt Mary. 'You were no virgin Mary before you were married, you know. You're no better than nobody. I seen the time when you were glad to borrow a bit of bread. Stickie Dickie, that's what they called you at school.'

'Shut up Aunt Mary,' Ralph shouts down the stairs. 'It's nobody to blame.'

'Your Ma's no more religious than my arse,' Aunt Mary shouts and pulls the door closed. Then she opens it again.

'Why don't you bugger off and get a job instead of painting filthy girls with nothing on? Why don't you earn an honest wage?' she shouts. We go downstairs. There's a few people hanging round our gate. Aunt Mary sticks her head in the door again. 'Will I tell the neighbours about the time you pissed in a bucket behind the door?' She laughed and Derek kicked the door closed in her face. We heard her go out of the gate, still laughing.

'I didn't think she would turn out like that,' I say.

'They're all a bit mad,' Derek says. 'Madness runs in this family on both sides.'

'She's maybe not all that bad,' Ralph says.

'God,' Derek says. 'Who does he think he is? Jasus.'

'I just think it's hard to get to understand what's in some people's minds,' Ralph says.

There was a thud, thud, thud on the floor and we went up; it was Ma. She had her clothes off and was in bed.

'What's up?' Derek asks. She was lying holding her head.

'Will you bring me up a glass of water and a couple of Aspros?' she said. She was putting on a trembling voice. Ralph went down and got the things. Her hands shook so that the water spilt all over the bed. Then she swallowed the Aspros and she stopped shaking and her voice was all right too.

'Has your Aunt Mary gone?' she asks.

'She's gone all right,' Derek says. 'And left us with an extra mouth to feed.'

'What?' Ma says. 'Where is he?'

'He's still in the bathroom,' Ralph says.

'Somebody better run after her and tell her to take him. In God's name, run,' Ma says. She threw her legs out of the bed and pulled on a dress.

The boy was still wet but Derek took his hand and dragged him down through the new houses and up the road, but he never caught up with Aunt Mary, although he said he ran as fast as he could with the dim-witted boy dragging onto his arm. He had to bring him back.

When they came back Da was in. He was fed up listening to Ma going on and on about Aunt Mary, telling him about the bath being cracked and the toilet seat, but Da kept rubbing his stomach, saying, 'Aye well I'll hear all about that when I eat my dinner,' but Ma said how did he expect a dinner to be ready after a day like that. She said it was all right for Da to go out to work every day and have no worries. He met nice, smiling people all day, but she had to face the neighbours when things like that happened. Wasn't there no mercy for her? She kept on to Da to go up and see the bathroom, but he wouldn't move. He said his stomach was sore and Ma asked him what he thought her head was like. He was lucky seeing smiling faces all day at work. Half the married women nowadays were out at work, but she never left her children to go to work, to buy lipstick and records, she wouldn't leave children to roam the countryside and maybe get killed by a train or drowned. God gave her the health to look after them, but what thanks did she get for it. They did damn all for her.

Da said that would do for a sermon and could she just

make some tea and a bit of bread. Ma said that her mother would turn in her grave if she heard the language that Aunt Mary was coming out with. Aunt Mary was Ma's half-sister and Ma and her never got on. Ma said that when Wendy was lying around she was just the spit and image of Aunt Mary. That Aunt Mary would never be dead while Wendy was alive. Aunt Mary wouldn't wash a dish, she was so spoilt. Her Ma did everything for her and she got no thanks. Not even when she died washing Aunt Mary's dress. Da said he heard all that a thousand times before. If he only had a cup of tea and a bit of bread. It wasn't much to ask for after being out at work all day to try and get money to pay the rent. Ma said that's all she was: a slave for cleaning the house and making food.

Then when Derek brought back the dim-witted boy she asked Da what he was going to do about it. She made Da some tea and he had to ride away up to the country to ask Aunt Mary to come and take him back. Ma said she wondered what wrong Aunt Mary had done before the eyes of God to get a son like that. She said after hearing Aunt Mary's bad language today maybe it was better that he was stupid. The boy sat and blew bubbles in the tea and kept filling the cup with sugar. He had to wear one of Wendy's dresses because we couldn't get anything else to fit him. Derek thought that was the biggest laugh and kept putting his arm round him and running his hand up his leg. That was all right for a while, but the boy wanted to touch Derek. He wanted to feel his hands and stick his fingers in Derek's mouth. Derek got annoyed after a while and let on he was going to hit him over the head with the brush.

When Da came home and told us that Aunt Mary wouldn't let him in, she wouldn't even listen to what he had to say, Ma said that he should be put into a home or a hospital where they understood things like that. Ralph

74

said the only difference between him and us was that he was slower, it took him ten years to learn what we could learn in one year. 'That's all right,' Da says. He was trying to have a serious discussion with Ralph. 'That's okay,' he said. 'If we all learnt ten years behind, then he would be as wise as us.'

'True enough,' Ralph says. 'But we're all different.'

'No we're not,' Da says. 'Now we're not, but in the beginning if he had learnt the same as us, then he wouldn't be like that.'

'Where did you get that nonsense from,' Ralph says. 'From the Bible, you believe that about we're all evil?' The dim-witted boy sat staring at the fire as if his eyes and body were frozen. As if there was something pressing on his head. Derek put his hand down quick in front of his eyes to see if he could make him blink, but his eyes stared straight at the fire.

'There's no good trying to have a wise conversation with him,' Ma said to Da. 'He'll have to try and pull down the teachings of Christ that made him.'

'Wait a minute,' Da says. 'I see what he means.' He leans back and folds his arms. 'You got a point there.'

'You see,' Ralph says. 'If we were all the same in every way, then we might as well be dead.'

'It might be a better world if people were the same,' Da says. 'They might be less trouble.'

'No.' Ralph says. 'Contrast keeps us alive. I mean these houses are all the same. You might as well live in one as eleven and if you go for a walk you might as well stop at one.'

'You're going away off the subject now,' Da says. 'Stick to the point.'

'A'm trying to explain to you,' Ralph says.

'No you're not,' Da says.

'You don't follow me,' Ralph says.

'I know you're talking a lot of nonsense,' Da says. 'You got these fool ideas in your head.'

'Here we start again. Never a night goes by but there's a row in this house,' Ma says. 'Then it's me that faces the neighbours the next day.'

'I hate people that would argue a black crow was white,' Da says. 'It must be that teacher that learns you to be stupid. You would think the way you and him talk you knew it all.'

'Well argue away up to bed,' Ma says.

Wendy had come in late and was reading a love story in one of Ma's magazines. Derek wouldn't give her peace. He was telling her that we had got a boy for her. The boy was still staring at the fire, not caring whether he was wearing Wendy's blue dress or not. It was a cotton dress and there was a little worn out bit where someone had been for a long time trying to stick their finger through, when Wendy was wearing it.

'Do you see those murderer's eyes?' Derek said to Wendy.

'You would think he is only eight or nine, but he's about thirty and he's a killer.' The boy put his head back and let it stay there. His mouth was open and he was still staring at the fire.

'You see,' Derek says to Wendy. 'He tries to kiss you with his mouth open like that and do you know what he does if you don't let him?'

'Shut up,' Wendy says in a mournful kind of voice.

'He puts his thumbs on your eyeballs and presses them into your brain.'

'Shut up,' Wendy shouts.

'He crawls into your room when you're asleep and lies beside you feeling all over his face and making fearful howling sounds.'

'Ma, tell him to shut up,' Wendy says, in a cry-like sound.

'If you would get away up to bed then he wouldn't keep you going,' Ma says. She gets up and stands near Wendy.

'What's that rubbish you're reading?' In the book there was a picture of some film star kissing a lovely girl. She had her blouse open and hung over her shoulder, but you couldn't see the man's hands.

'It's an interesting story,' Wendy says.

'You would rather read these stories on love or some filthy stuff instead of reading the Bible before you go to bed,' Ma says.

Ma said she couldn't put the boy out in the street, so at least he could stay for one night. Derek didn't want him to stay upstairs. Anyway there was no bed for him, so Ma made the sofa comfortable for him with a few good heavy blankets. It was difficult to get him to lie down. Derek spoke to him like a dog, saying, 'Down boy, lie, lie.' But it made no difference. As soon as we went to go up the stairs, he got up again. Ma tried to say a prayer to him, but that was no good either. In the end we just put out the light and shut the door, and if he wanted to roam around the kitchen all night it was up to him. We all closed the room doors before we got into bed. Other nights we left the doors open so that we could shout in to each other's room. Ma got up in the middle of the night, because she thought she heard the bath running, but it wasn't him, it was only her imagination.

The next morning when I got up to go to work he was still lying on the sofa, still with the blue dress on.

Next day I had to be initiated, even though the plaster was still over the top of my eye. I didn't put up much of a struggle this time. They got me when I was sitting under the vats having a smoke. The ginger boy whom I had the fight with was there too, but he wasn't so bad, he just kept an eye in case Bob Wright would come or any of the governors.

When they got me on my back on the floor I couldn't do much. I couldn't see what was going on, but I could feel them opening my belt and then my fly. I kicked a bit then but it was no good, they had made up their minds to really do it this time. I felt my trousers coming down, then I knew they could see it. Some of them were laughing.

'It's not bad for his age,' one of them said.

'Should we make it stand?' another one said and I could feel him pulling at it.

It was frightening because I thought they were going to cut it off when one of them said, 'He would be safer without that thing.' I put up a bit of a fight then, but they still had a good hold on me. Then they were all laughing and I was lying there feeling somebody rubbing something on me. One boy snorted like a horse and whoever was rubbing the stuff on me was laughing too, because I could feel his hands vibrating. They didn't button my trousers up; they just all let go when they had finished.

Right over my belly and all over my penis was thick grease. They stood around laughing while I pulled my underpants over the thickly greased skin and buttoned up my trousers. I felt terrible; to go to the toilet I had to go through a room full of women and men with white aprons on. I got the feeling that they all knew that I had just been initiated. My pants felt as if they were sliding down all the time. A big fat woman called me over and gave me a sweet. Then she asked me if I had a girl friend. I said I hadn't and she asked me if I wanted her to put in a good word for me with one of the girls in the room. Then she put her head down and said as if she wasn't talking to me, 'Look out, Look out.' There, coming along towards me, was Mr Andrews and another man. He was a little man with a stick and not too sure of his step. 'It's the Old Man himself,' the woman said. 'You better skedaddle quick.'

The Old Man had seen me. He had yellow looking eyes

and his skin looked like new skin that grows over a big cut, or if you have boils taken away and the skin never grows smooth again. I knew as soon as I looked at him that I disliked him. 'I'll stand my ground,' I say. The woman carried on working. They came right across to me. The Old Man stood there like a dying hen. His skin was worse than I had first thought. He had a very bitter look and there were wide spaces between his brown teeth.

'What are you doing here, young man?' he says.

'Going to wash my prick,' I say and walked off and left him.

The toilet frightened me. There were four doors, with nothing to say whether anyone was in there or not: you could hear the sound of running water all the time. I tried the first door, it opened a bit then someone pushed it closed again. I didn't know whether to try any of the other doors or not. Three men stood smoking. I leant up against the whitewashed wall and lit a butt. The three men had white aprons on and one had a big cap that sat on his ears and he kept looking at me. I didn't like to look at him because he had a big red lump on the side of his face. He threw his cigarette end down the place where the piss ran down the drain and stuck both hands in his pockets and went out. After he went out, the other two men started talking about him.

'He wouldn't give you the skin of his fart,' the dark-skinned man says.

'Who, your man?' the other says. He was a grey-haired man and his skin was grey too.

The dark-coloured man turned his back on me and mumbles to the other one, 'He's odd, odd as hell.'

'I see that,' the other man says. 'He wouldn't stay and wait for you. He just finishes his fag and goes, even if you're on your own.'

'Aye and he sits by himself to eat his lunch.'

'He would lick old Andrew's arse for a bit of overtime.'

They both finish their cigarettes and go. I hang around a bit before trying another door. I can hear two people talking in the top two boxes, so I try the third one down. Scored on the door is BE A MAN AND NOT A FOOL, PULL THE CHAIN AND NOT YOUR TOOL. Signed at the bottom is SHAKESPEAR.

What a place : there was just a big board to sit on and the river ran underneath. It wasn't very firm because there was nothing to hold it except a ledge that it rested on at each end. Dividing each box was a panel of thin plywood. There was no toilet paper, just squares of newspaper tied onto the door. I took down my trousers. There was grease all over me. I dried off what I could with the newspaper; then I thought I could wet my handkerchief. The river was low, I leant over the board and tried to touch the water. The board suddenly jolted out of place and there was a splash. It was right down into the water at one end, but I held onto it and only my arms got wet. I could only hear the confusion of spluttering and coughing and shouting. I was almost upside down, but I could keep my head out of the water by holding onto the plank. When I looked through into the other boxes I could just see a big bare behind : the man was clinging onto something with one hand and trying to pull up his wet trousers with the other hand and as far as I could see he had his feet on the plank, but it was deeper in the water at that end. Further up I could see a bald head sticking out of the water; to my right someone was sitting on the plank, it was well out of the water at that end. A cap came floating round my arms. It touched my arms and spun round slow, then went on down. The backside to my right jumped up and down a bit, trying to rise, then before any of us knew where we were, we were all right in the water. The plank had slid off the ledge at that side too. It was cold, but not too deep, my head was just below the toilet floor level. There was a lot of people looking down in at us.

'Somebody give me a hand,' I says.

'Shut up,' the litte man with the bald head says.

He didn't seem to want to get out; the man that fell in last was already climbing out, his trousers hanging down at his ankles and him not able to bend his knees up onto the floor. Then somebody pulled him straight out. The other man must have got out just as I went down, because he wasn't there any more. Somebody reached for the bald-headed man, but he says, 'Let go.' The hand tried to catch him, but he moved back.

Then I heard someone say, 'He won't come out without his cap,' and someone else say, 'It's gone down the river now.'

'Let him stay there,' another man says. I was able to pull my trousers up while I was standing in the water and two men took my arms and I got out okay.

'Go to the yarn loft,' one of the men tells me, 'You'll get dried out there.' I wanted to get away as soon as possible so I didn't bother to ask where it was. I thought it must be somewhere that I had never been before, so instead of going back the way I come I went round the yard. It was very cold. My wellingtons were sucking at my feet and the wet clothes were like ice against my skin. Round the corner there was a big long building and I had just walked down a bit when I realized that it was full of young girls. They started to shout out the window at me. The place must have been crammed full of them because in no time there was half-a-dozen hanging out of each window looking and screaming. 'Take anybody with you,' one girl shouted and everybody laughed.

Then another shouted, 'Did you piss yourself love?' Her voice was loud and screechy. That got the best laugh. Each time I come down towards a window all I could see was the mass of faces looking at me and they were looking at me from behind. I could tell that they were watching every step I took and my trousers wrinkling up and down my hips. 'Is it long since?' one girl shouts.

Then another shouts, 'You mean is it long.' They were all hysterical. I could feel myself wanting to pee. I tried to go faster, but the wellingtons seemed just to go at their own speed. I felt the warm pee running between my legs. I didn't want to look down, but I was sure they couldn't tell I was doing it. As soon as I got to the bottom of the building I did 'up you' with my fingers and they roared louder than ever. Then I did it again and turned round the corner quick and the roar died down. The Old Man was standing with Jim Smith and I didn't see them till I was on them; they were standing apart and I couldn't make up my mind whether to go between them or round them, but they both looked at me and I stopped. The Old Man signalled me over with his finger and didn't move his feet at all. His head quivered as he spoke. His old skin was loose round his mouth.

'We don't have time for boys like you here,' he says and looked at Jim Smith. Jim Smith nodded his approval. 'Next time we find you fooling around with the young ladies we will have to ask you to take a little walk home.' His voice got a little louder. 'And stay there,' he says.

'It was them,' I say.

'What were you doing down this yard?' he says.

'Looking for the yarn loft,' I say. 'I need to get dried.'

'You will have to go back the way you came,' he says and him and Jim Smith walk off together. I didn't want to go back past those girls again – so I hurried past them.

'Come here young man,' the Old Man said. I turned and although I was really cold with the wet clothes, my whole head got hot with anger, him standing there with his expensive suit on – under his clothes he would just be ugly and human, not much better than an animal, flesh and blood and skin and shit.

'Round the other way,' Jim Smith said in a firm voice.

'We haven't got time to waste on you,' the Old Man said. 'You do what you're told or get out.'

I go back past the women, but I don't want to. I know myself and that Old Man is no better than I am : he's only flesh and blood like Jim Smith and me too, but Jim Smith would lick his arse; he's no wiser than I am : he has a lot of money, that's all. Ma and Da are no wiser than I am, because Da can't understand Ma and she can't understand him and nobody can understand Ralph.

Those two men know as little as me, telling me what to do like Ma and Da used to. I understand Ralph a bit and I could say he's right or I could say he's wrong. It's better to say nothing because I don't know. If you're right or if you're wrong doesn't matter, if he knows his mind and knows best.

I didn't know I broke the window, I didn't even see YARN HOUSE written up above the bit that wasn't broken. I opened the door and went in, my hand wasn't cut and nobody seen me as far as I know, because I have to go through another door, but I broke that window all the same, I knew as soon as I did it, it was me. Like that time at school. We were just standing around, two or three of us. We were in the teacher's end then. It was near Christmas and she had made a big round hut out of plaster, to show us how the Eskimoes live and I broke it, but I didn't know I did, but I think she must have been right because I was the nearest to it and she caned me.

I went through the other door and up the stairs. There was a man with thick frizzy hair sliding bales of yarn down a shute. A girl was tying labels on them; every time the man went to take a bale from her he caught her breast and she pushed at him and he laughed, neighed like a horse. 'Oh here's another drowned rat,' he says, when I went over to him. Then he catches the girl and pushes her down onto a lot of old waste yarn that was in a corner. He held her down. She shouts, 'I'll pull your hair,' but he has a firm grip on both her arms.

'Do you want to see a bit of leg?' he says to me. His face is thin and red and he has no teeth. She has long red hair and her face is freckled. He puts one hand down quick and pulls her overall up, but not far enough for me to see her knickers. She kicks and shouts, 'You dirty bugger,' then he gets right on top of her and kisses her hard; after that he stands up and spits on his hands.

'Treat them rough, they like that,' he says. She sits up and straightens her hair with her hands.

'Can't you see the young fellow's wet,' she says. Her voice is a bit shaky.

'You want to see him taking his clothes off,' he says. 'You want to see his wee willie.'

'I want to get dried out,' I say.

'We'll soon fix that,' he says. 'But maybe you would like a wee bit at this girl first.' He neighs for a long time. A little smile comes over her face.

'You're embarrassing the young fellow,' she says.

'It would take more than that to embarrass that fellow,' he says and picked up a brown coat. 'Follow me,' he says.

We went into a big room or a kind of oven the size of a room. The light was dim. There were skeins and skeins of all different coloured yarns hanging from the ceiling.

'This is the drying room, I'll leave you to it. Just take your clothes off and hang them over one of them beams and you can put this coat on meantime, in case somebody sees your wee willie.' He went further up in, then I saw the little bald-headed man sitting on a box with a brown coat on too. He was wearing a cap now but it wasn't the one I saw floating on the water.

'This boy will keep you company,' the frizzy-haired man said and went out through a door at the other end.

The little bald man had white hairy legs and there was no

space between his toes: they were more or less one solid toe. I took off my clothes and he watched me all the time. When I put on the brown coat and sat on the box beside him he was very talkative.

'That's not a bad one you've got there for your age,' he said, peering at me as if he could see through the brown coat I was wearing.

'It's all right,' I say. 'At school mine was the biggest in my class.' He had a habit of making little blowing noises from his nose and little noises like he was clearing his throat.

'Mmm,' he says. 'It would soon shrink when it hit the cold water.' When he looked right round at me I noticed for the first time that he had a hole through one of his cheeks. It looked like a hole that had been there a long time and yellow stuff had almost hardened in there.

'Your name's not Ned Robinson?' I asked him.

'How did you know?' He looked at me inquiringly. I didn't like to say, because Da had told me about a man called Ned Robinson who tried to shoot himself but only made a hole in his cheek.

'That frizzy-haired man told me,' I say. He looked at me doubtfully, then he nodded his head as much as to say, it doesn't matter anyway.

'This is the day the cow calves,' he says.

'What does that mean?' I ask.

'The day they hand out the money,' he says. 'Pay day.'

'For all you get,' I says. 'They give it to you in one hand and take it off you in the other.' I only said that because Da always said it. So then I say, 'Maybe that's true and maybe it's not.'

'What will you spend your money on?' he says, then he whispered into my ear. 'A wee girl.'

'I don't know,' I said. 'Maybe I'll have to give it to Ma.'

There was a very dry heat in the room and the snot in my

nose had dried up. I thought that the heat had also dried the stuff coming out of the hole in his cheek.

'Have you ever had a wee girl?' he asks me and looked round to make sure the room was still empty.

'I had,' I say.

'You had.'

'I had a lot of times,' I say.

'Boy's a dear,' he says. 'And what age are you?'

'Fourteen,' I says.

'Oh it's nice,' he says. 'What was the last wee girl like?'

'It was the time the concert was on in the village,' I said. 'I was standing at the corner, just looking at everybody going home. This this girl came past, she was lovely, she had a nice coat on. Her face was lovely and she had nice curly hair.' Ned was really interested.

'Go on,' he says.

'I said to her, "Hello beautiful", and she said to me, "Hello love" and then she kind of stopped and I said, "Are you taking anybody with you?" and then she walked away and said, "I might".'

'Did you go?' he asked and fingered inside his pocket.

'I did – after she was away up the street a bit, I followed her. Then I put my arm round her shoulder – just joking and she put her arm round me too.' I looked at Ned and he was sitting in a kind of trance listening hard. 'Her and me went over the field. You know it's a short cut to our house and she lived in the same estate.'

'Go on,' he says, impatiently.

'It was misty. We could hardly see where we were going. Then we fell over them stones and I kissed her, then when I got up she still lay there.'

'Oh, man, sir. It was biting the leg of her,' Ned said. Fumbling more now with his hands in the coat pocket, pulling it all into a wisp between his legs.

'That was okay,' I say.

'Did she let you?' he asks.

'Not at first,' I say.

'Once you get them going they let you,' he says. 'Man, they love it, they love it as much as men.' Then he put his head forward towards mine as if he was asking me a big secret. 'Did you like it?'

'Do you do it sometimes?' I ask.

'Man, sir, do I what?' he says and gives a little nervous giggle. His mouth is just a small slit in his face and I can only see the line where his teeth meet, the rest of his face is flat. When I look at him, he covers the little giggle with his hand and clears his throat. 'Man, sir, I love it.' he says. 'I love it with wee young girls.'

'How do you get them?' I ask. I wanted him to tell me now, I was starting to be aroused. His words were real dreams in my head.

'I spend a wee bit of time in the evenings mending clocks you know, just for the people round about. I was fixing a clock one night when I heard this wee knock on the door, who could that be, says I to myself. "Come in," I shouts. It was this wee girl, man, she was lovely. She had big brown eyes and lovely wavy hair. I never seen a girl like her. She must have been only about thirteen. "What can I do for ye," I says. Then I says, "If I were younger I know what I would do." Her wee face went as red as a beetroot. "It's my Da's clock. He needs it for the morning and the alarm'll not go off."

' "A'm a bit pushed for time," I say. "But come over here and sit beside me and I'll have a look at it." She blushed and come over and sat down near to me. She had lovely fat legs. "The clock isn't worth fixing. I'd lend him one to keep him going for a day or two," I says, then I picked up my own clock and put it on her knee. "Thanks," she says and sat on. Then I started to show her how to work it and all the time I rubbed her wee leg.

' "You pull that wee thing out after you set it. Make sure you do or it'll not go off in the morning," I says to her. After a bit I noticed that her legs opened a bit then closed. "Ye needn't be scared of me," I says to her. "I could be your grandfather." She relaxed and I ran me hand right between her legs. She gave a sigh and lay back.'

He was going on and on as if it was all happening in his head now and I sat letting go into my head too.

'They went right open. I just eased her up and slipped her wee pants off. Man, sir, there wasn't a hair on it. We both got down on the sofa – ah never seen a wee girl enjoy it so much – she cried and held on to me. That wee soft body of hers just gasping and her eyes closed for a long time after it. As if it was still going on. Man, sir, she was round with a different clock every night after that.'

We both sat silent : the heat of the room seemed to make the juice run out of our brains. The dry air was still; suddenly the door clattered open and the frizzy-haired man come in.

'Are you two loafers going to get your pay?' he said, going over and feeling our clothes. 'They're dry now, if you want to put them on.'

My mouth was full of sleep. We got up and felt the clothes – they had dried stiff.

'We better get these on,' Ned says. 'This will never pay the rent.' The frizzy-haired man give a great neigh of a laugh and went out.

We had to go to Jim Smith's office for our pay. It was the young girl who was paying out through a hatch. We all stood in a line against the wall; every time somebody signed for their pay packet one of the men at the back made a remark like : 'Don't spend it all in the one shop,' or, 'The wife will be glad to see that.' One man at the back always shouted, 'Ah give it them back,' and everybody chuckled. He laughed every time he said it too. He had a laugh like a sheep and two or three of the bleach boys always imitated him, but he didn't realize it. He looked pleased with himself.

When I went to sign for mine the girl says, 'Just a minute' and went to the back where Jim Smith was sitting. He left down his pen and nodded his head to her.

'Mr Smith would like to see you,' she says. I signed for the packet and went into the office.

'I'll come straight to the point,' Jim Smith says. 'Why did you break the window in the door to the yarn house? Come on now. Was it to show your hatred for Mr Andrews senior. Hmm?'

'Who said I broke it?' I say.

'Never mind that,' he says. 'We know it was you. Why?'

'I don't know,' I say. 'I just done it.'

He lay back in his chair. 'Come off it son, we can't waste time and money like this, there must have been a reason.'

'I don't know any reason,' I say. 'I just did it.' That was as true as I could say.

'We expect you to pay for the new glass,' he says. 'And Mr Andrews senior expects an apology.'

When I came out of the office, all the men who had been queuing up for their pay had gone home. The big yard was empty. I got a funny feeling looking through the grey air. It looked as if everybody had gone home except Jim Smith and me. He reminded me of a thin red rat who had eaten the whole place clean and silent like the last man left in the world, but if I killed him there would be nothing left. I tried to put that thought out of my mind. Was there anything to live for? One stinking man. Maybe everybody is like him. If I could see into their brains, I might kill myself: I can sometimes – old Ned Robinson, I saw every trace in his mind when he was telling me about what he did to the little girl. He was like a cow with cud, vomiting the same fading pictures into his mind, trying to squeeze more and more life juice through his body. I can see Ralph's mind working: there's a strong feeling in his blood, he doesn't know why; it is fear and he says it's beauty. He calls those big trees he paints beauty. He calls naked hairless babies love and that big picture he did of nothing was fear too. He said it gave him a feeling of truth; maybe it did, but he didn't know nothing. He just knew that he thought it wasn't getting closer to fear, to nothing, but the thing in him that curdles like steel between his legs is too strong, it has got tight and is sleeping all through his body and his mind. It makes him kiss the dim-witted boy, because it just goes through and through him and it doesn't know what it wants, only to get out. Wendy has it strong too, but it stays more in the one place. It stays in her head and between her legs. She just lies there curled up on the sofa, like it was just coming out of the ground and going through her tickling and curdling nice against her inside. Derek wants to turn everything inside out; that's why he's mad, because he knows it's there, like feathers in his blood, but he wants to see it. He's not allowed, because if God were turned inside out, Derek would be God.

The Old Man's office is near the bleach. The door is locked; if he had been there, I would have said sorry. God knows why. I might have said to him are you real, or are you just that bad skin?

There is just a pound in my pay packet; I put it into my hip pocket and get on the bike. The bike is cold and the air is cold and miserable.

When I get down into the village, just as I come up towards

90

the Hog's Head I see the dim-witted boy. He is standing below the window. There's an old dog half-sitting, half-lying against the wall, like it had just come out of the pub and maybe would be sick if it didn't keep its eyes open. I put the bike beside the pub door. The light is on inside and there's a strong, cold smell of stout coming out. The boy is looking at the dog under his glasses and the dog is looking at him. There is a yellow wax in the corner of its eyes and the whites of its eyes are almost yellow, like old newspaper. The boy doesn't look at me. He just keeps on staring at the dog under his glasses. The dog blinks and looks down as if it were getting tired, then it starts staring back at him again, like they were both amazed that they couldn't see into each other's minds. The boy has his own clothes on again.

'Who brought you here?' I say, but he doesn't answer. He turns his head slow towards the pub door.

'Is there anybody you know in there?' I say. The dog looks around slow. There's a policeman coming down the street. He's walking like a cowboy, the old woman who lives near the Police Station is with him, they call her Foxie for a nickname. Some people call her *The News of the World*. She looks at somebody going past on his bike. Her head turns round quick and she says something to the policeman. He doesn't look at her: he is looking at the dim-witted boy.

'It has been here all day,' she was saying, 'there must be something wrong with it,' but the policeman doesn't look at the dog. He is looking at the boy all the time.

'It must be sick,' the woman was saying, but she was looking at the boy too.

'Would that be your Aunt Mary's wee boy?' she says to me.

'That's what they tell me,' I say. 'But it's nobody's business.' The policeman is bending down slow beside the dog.

He is grinning all the time, as if he were laughing at everybody. As if he were the only wise person.

'It must be very sick, it has been sitting there all day,' the woman says. The boy and the dog are still staring at each other. The policeman takes out his gun and holds it to the dog's ear and shoots the bullet right into its head. It just falls. The boy doesn't even jump at the bang.

'You didn't know whether it was going to die or not,' I say.

'I knew as soon as I took my gun out,' the policeman says, straightening up.

'It was well for it,' the woman says.

'How do you know?' I say.

The policeman caught the dog by the hind-legs and dragged it up the street. The woman stood and looked at the boy. Her eyes moved fast like a wild animal's and her lips stuck out like she was wearing gum-shields. A few men were standing at the pub door now. Her eyes moved fast into them, looking them up and down, almost looking through them.

'What's the bang, lady?' one of the men says in a slurred voice. His cap was pushed well back on his head and his hair was blue. He moved out onto the footpath like a child learning to walk; there was wet down the side of his trousers. He stood unsteadily in his big wellingtons, almost falling forwards, then almost falling backwards. The woman moved back, making sure she was out of his reach.

'Is this all you can do? You should be ashamed of yourself and I feel for your nice wife and children,' she says.

'There's no bitch going to tell me how to spend my money.' He swayed back and pointed his finger at her. 'If I ever need your advice missus, I'll ask for it.'

'It's got nothing to do with me,' she says. 'It's the children and your lovely wife I'm thinking about.'

'You're a nosy old bitch,' he says. 'And everybody knows it. You stick your neb in everything.'

'Rab, will you come in here, she's not worth bothering about,' one of the men at the door shouts. He looks round. He turns his whole body round, but his feet stay in the same place. 'You fine men standing there, loyal friends, you know there's not a word of truth in what she says.' He puts up his hand. 'Did ever any of you see my children going hungry?'

'You've been drinking all day,' the woman says.

'Will you deprive me of the only thing I've got in life, a packet of cigarettes and a bottle or two of stout? Hmm, what else can a man live for?' He falls up against the wall and lies there.

'It's the Lord up above to judge,' she says. 'It's between you and your maker.'

'Missus.' He rolls against the wall. 'Missus, far be it for me to destroy anybody's faith, but the man up above has never give me much chance to have faith in Him.' He looked at the dim-witted boy. 'If there's a God, why are there children born like this?' He rolled off the wall over towards me. 'Forgive me, son, for speaking like that about your friend, but I mean no harm to him.'

'That's okay,' I say.

'He's suffering for the sins of his parents,' the woman says and goes to walk away. Then she says, 'If you had looked after your dog, it wouldn't be dead now.'

'Explain yourself missus,' he says, but he knew, he knew now the bang he heard was his old dog getting shot. The woman walked away, her head poking out in front of her.

'Explain yourself missus,' he shouts and slides down the wall. The next thing I seen Ralph come out of the pub, he goes and tries to pull the man up. The man's face is wrinkled, his eyes are soft and slippery looking. He holds his arm round Ralph's shoulder, Ralph tries to lift him; his body comes up a bit but his legs are still on the ground and his head is hanging down too. There's only the whites of his eyes to be seen, his mouth is open and he brings up a little brown curdled slime.

'Somebody help me get him up,' Ralph says. He is trying to lift him, but he's too heavy. Two men came out and took his arms and put them round their necks, then they lifted him easily.

'Let the woman explain herself,' he says.

The two men talked to him like he was a child. 'You're all right Rab, take it easy now man.'

'I'm all right,' he says. 'I never ask anybody to buy my drink. The money I spend's my own.'

'Pay no attention to what that old bag says,' the men were saying. 'We have been friends for a long time now Rab, we know you're good to your children, you've got a big heart, Rab.'

They stagger into the pub. Ralph looks at me. 'He had too much, but he'll be all right. Is it true they shot his old dog?'

'I seen the policeman do it,' I says.

'It was okay,' Ralph says. 'It didn't need to be shot, it would have pulled through all right.'

'I know that only too well,' I says.

'If it's dead now, there's nothing to be done,' Ralph says. 'But what right have the police got, they think they're God Almighty. What do they know about the mind of a dog?'

'She said it was well for it,' I say.

'How does she know?'

'That's what I asked her,' I say. 'It would have been better to let it live just to see.'

'Who knows what's best,' Ralph says.

The dim-witted boy was looking at Ralph as if he was trying to sort out every word Ralph spoke.

'Were you drinking?' I ask.

'I just went in for a bottle,' Ralph says.

'Does Ma know?' I ask him.

'No,' he says. 'At the age I am now, there's no need to tell her everything.'

'She doesn't like it,' I say. 'She'll kick up hell if she knows about it.'

'She'd kick up hell if you were doing anything you were enjoying. Even if it was only picking your nose,' Ralph says.

'I never heard you talk like that,' I say, because his voice is louder than usual. 'Maybe you had more than one?'

'No,' he says. 'It's just that a'm fed up with the whole set up. What can you do? If you enjoy something, you're going to go to hell, or kill yourself; if you don't think the same as other people they get angry, they want you to be the same; if you are the same, they all say you should be different, not to follow, they get annoyed if you say the same thing.' The dim-witted boy kept watching Ralph's mouth.

'I never seen you go on like this before Ralph,' I say. 'Are you drunk?'

'Come in,' he says. 'And get a bottle of lemonade.'

'What about the boy?' I say.

'He can come in too,' Ralph says. 'When that dog was here, he wouldn't come in, he wanted to stay outside with it.' Ralph held out his hand and the dim-witted boy took it and followed Ralph in.

There was a line of men leaning up against the counter. Ralph nodded to them and they nodded back like they knew him well. One or two of them made remarks about Ralph being an artist. The bar was long and narrow, the counter was painted bright red and halfway down the walls were painted royal blue while the bottom-half was whitewashed. The dim-witted boy followed Ralph right up through. Everybody tried to look away from him and I tried to let on that I wasn't coming in with them.

We went through a door at the far end; inside there was a big open fire burning. Ralph stopped inside the door.

'You see these men here,' he whispered. 'A lot of folk

think they're stupid, but these men know all about art and books and that kind of thing.'

'I can believe it,' I say. He scratches his head self-consciously because he thinks the men might have heard what he had said.

I knew most of the men in the room by sight and I knew a bit about them too. Ma wasn't right into the new house before she was able to tell Da a bit about somebody, that's how I knew most of what I knew. She had no respect for anybody who went into the pub. There was two students in the village who were studying law. Ma always gave them as an example : 'Did anybody ever see them go into the pub? No, well them boys could show you how to live a good clean life.'

One man sat on a low chair at the side of the fire : his legs were crossed and they came up under his chin. He had a big bottle of red wine down at the side of his feet and every now and then he groped down with his large hand without looking to make sure it was still there. The rest of the men were drinking stout out of glasses, but he was drinking red wine out of a tin mug. He had a big, long, sad-looking face with the corners of his mouth drooping down low at each side. It would have almost made you cry to look at him. Hugh Gape was his name; he had been adopted by his two aunts. Ma said he was no good, his aunts were good to him, but he never forgave them for adopting him. He was twenty-five before they told him that neither of them was his mother; after that he took a rope and went out to the shed to hang himself. They said if he came in and sat by the fire they would buy him a bicycle. That stopped him from killing himself that time, but later on he was going to throw himself in the river unless they would buy him a motor bicycle. The old aunts worked their fingers to the bone to get him everything – to keep him from getting angry. One night one of them got very ill; she told him she was going to die, and he held up his fist and shouted that if she died he would kill her. Ma said that was the only thing that kept her alive, she lived for him for three months after that. He was able to drink every day and he never did a day's work in his life. Ma said a boy like that should get jail. Ralph said that half the things they said about him weren't true.

When he saw Ralph he uncrossed his big legs slowly and stood up. Ralph went over to him and they shook hands, like they hadn't seen each other for years.

'You're all right Hugh,' Ralph says in a real friendly voice.

'Say nothing, whatever you say, say nothing.' He looked round the room as if he had just spoken great words of wisdom; then he tried to ease himself down into the low chair again.

'You're all right Hugh,' Ralph says and they still had a firm grip on each other's hands; then he half got up and looked round the room again.

'A boy's best friend's his mother,' he says and Ralph helped him ease back down into the chair.

'You're all right Hugh,' Ralph says again in a consoling voice, the way you would talk to a child.

The dim-witted boy sat down on the low chair at the other side of the fire. Hugh put up his hand to him in a friendly gesture, then when he saw him sitting there with his mouth hanging open he could see that he was dim-witted and didn't know what to do. The boy just looked at the fire except when Ralph went to go away to sit at the table where the other men were sitting. Then he got up to follow Ralph.

'He's coming after you,' I say to Ralph.

Ralph puts his hand on his shoulder and says, 'Come on now son, sit down here where you'll be warm.'

We went off to the top of the table. There was a special big chair for Ralph. I sat on one of the benches where the men were sitting in a row down both sides of the table.

Ralph sat back on the big chair like he was a king and all the men looked towards him. There was no tablecloth on the table, just scrubbed boards. In the middle there was a big oil-lamp with a long brass stem and at the top a big blue glass bowl half full of oil, the globe was long and thin and very clear.

'It looks like you've been in here a lot before,' I say to Ralph, but he didn't answer, he was sitting back in the chair like a peacock. His skin was brown and he had a little beard. Ma always told him there was nothing as nice as a nice clean-shaven fellow – like the news readers on TV. He didn't wear a tie either, just a brown corduroy shirt almost the same colour as his skin.

I knew most of the men round the table. One or two of them I had seen in River Side factory. There was Bertie Gloss; he had big ears. Da told about the time Bertie's wife showed somebody a photograph of him sitting on a chair. They said it was lovely and they liked the way the big wooden curls came out of the old fashioned chair. 'That's no wooden curls,' she said. 'That's Bertie's ears.' They weren't ordinary big ears; they sat out, you would think there was a strong wind behind him blowing them out all the time. At one time when he was younger they said he was in the I.R.A. and tried to blow up the Police Station.

At the bottom of the table was a big man with his cap thrown to the back of his head. They called him Kell's Water because every night when he was going home drunk he sang a song of that name. He sang: 'Here's health to Bonnie Kell's Water and long may it flow.' They said that sometimes he was seen drunk going to his work at eight o'clock in the morning, but Da said it was just the way he walked all the time.

The man beside him had a big white beard; he couldn't hold a job. One job he had was to look after the gates at the level crossing. He got a little house and free coal and electricity and all he had to do was to open the gates when he got the signal that the train was coming, but in one week the train went through the gates five times.

The fair-haired man at the other side of the table asked Ralph what he was going to have. Ralph said that he would have a bottle of stout. 'And you'll have a wee one with it,' he says.

'All right,' Ralph says. 'If you're sure that's all right.'

'Right,' the man says, 'and what's your friend having,' then he looks at me.

'That wouldn't be a brother of yours?' he says to Ralph.

'It is,' Ralph says. 'He better just have a lemonade.' Then the man looked at the dim-witted boy for a bit, but no words came.

'It's okay,' Ralph says, seeing that the man didn't know what to say. 'He'll have a lemonade too.'

The man looked embarrassed. 'I was just wondering who he is,' he says.

'That's a cousin of mine,' Ralph says, then he laughs. 'That's what they tell me anyway – but the devil O the one can tell for sure.' The men all down the table laughed.

'That reminds me,' Kell's Water says. 'About this man that said when his seventh son was born he had had enough, so he got the gun out and was going to shoot himself, then he took the gun away from his head and said. "No, why the hell should I? I might be shooting the wrong man." ' There was a roar of laughter and somebody called for drinks for the house.

Maggie, the landlady, come in and took the order. She seemed to know what everybody wanted, she brought it all in on a big tray and there was a bit of an argument about who would pay – everybody wanted to pay. Ralph brought out some money but somebody told him to stick it back in his pocket or they would never speak to him again. 'The artist is privileged,' somebody shouts. After everybody had full glasses, Ralph says:

'Well, folks, we've got a nice crowd here now and if there's anybody here who wants to speak, let him take this chair.'

There were shouts of 'No, No.' Then Maggie came in with some logs for the fire.

'I'll just put these logs on and then I won't disturb you gentlemen,' she says.

When she stooped to put the logs on, they all made remarks about her legs. She had thin legs with nylons hanging down round her feet. The big man at the side of the fire pretended to run his hand right up her leg, then he brought it away quick and stuck it into his pocket.

'Are you not wearing the mini-skirt yet Maggie?' he says.

She turned round and stood with her back to the fire. 'Gentlemen,' she says. 'I am not ashamed to tell you that I would not be seen dead in one of those mini-skirts, not that I think they are morally wrong, but I think they must be very cold. To tell you the truth, I still wear woolly underwear.'

'Hear, hear,' they all shout. 'Let me see it,' the big man at the fire shouts. They said that he had been to bed with her, but he denied it: he said she was still a virgin and fifty if she was a day. He told the men that she slept with her finger in it at night.

She gave the dim-witted boy a straw to suck his lemonade through and went out.

'Come on boy, what are you going to talk about tonight,' one of the men shouts to Ralph. As soon as Ralph opens his mouth they all say, 'Silence now, let the artist speak.'

'Well,' Ralph says, 'I'm only going to talk about the things we are trying to understand. In short, life and ourselves.' He took a long drink of stout and the room was silent except for the dim-witted boy sucking through the straw, with his mouth half open and more lemonade falling down the side of his chin than was going down his throat. Ralph left down the glass.

'What do we know? We know there's eggs and we know if you were to see an egg in the beginning and watch it going very fast, then you would see an egg in a duck's arse or in a human, then the next thing you would see it would crack – on its own. Then there would be a bird come out or a baby or something and before you would know where you were it would sprout up and lay a lot more eggs and then die and not be there any more, or if it is it's not the same as it was or maybe it is.'

The men all put their glasses back, leaving brown foam under their noses. Ralph took a long swig and finished his. In no time Maggie was in and had them filled again. When she was filling them up some of the men made signs behind her back with one finger. Ralph just laughed and Maggie took the empties out. All he said after was, 'It's a good life if you have a bottle and a good bit of crack. You need humour to get through. But you need to see the beauty around you too.'

I noticed that the big man at the side of the fire was filling the dim-witted boy's glass up with red wine and he was drinking it through the straw. I tried to tell Ralph, but he was too busy.

Soon everybody was talking. The man beside me asked Ralph a couple of questions, but everybody was asking questions and telling about things that had happened to them and between one thing and another I got drinking too. It was the man beside me who gave me some whisky. He was a nice man – very ugly, but very funny and friendly. He said he knew Da well. He worked with Da in River Side factory for a long time. I told him about the first time I saw Mr Andrews stick his finger in his arse and jump into the air. 'When he does that he's biting his nails,' he says.

'What do you mean?' I say.

'Well,' he says, 'when you see him doing that it means that he has swallowed his teeth and he's biting his nails.'

Later on he brought out a tin whistle and they all gathered round to listen to him. I felt good sitting beside him. I gave Ralph the pound and he bought him some whisky. Then we had a break and Kell's Water sang a song. He was well-oiled before he sang – he threw his cap on the floor and curled up in the corner. It looked like he was trying to back right through the corner at first, then he broke into song, his whole body moved – he jerked his shoulders to every word, like he was jerking the song out of his body. 'Here's health to Bonnie Kell's Water and may it never run dry.' The words he didn't know could only be heard as big mumbles coming through his nose. He got a good clap and if the man hadn't started up again on the tin whistle he would have sung it again.

The boy's eyes were like two balls of dirty melting ice running into each other now behind his glasses. Big Hugh and him seemed to have made friends, at least Big Hugh had made friends with him. While the music was playing he was trying to get the dim-witted boy to dance. Hugh was throwing his legs up and houghing. The boy was just walking and holding onto him. He still had some wine in his glass, but he couldn't suck it through the straw now, it had been chewed too much. Just then Bill, Maggie's brother, came in; he had a pub in the town too and they said that he owned the biggest part of the one in the village. He was always called out when rows had started. He was a well-dressed wee man with a white shirt and gold cuff-links and a gold tooth, it was to the side of his mouth and he had a habit of putting his mouth to the side to let people see it. He went straight over to Hugh. Hugh held his arm up to dance with him.

'Now that's enough,' he pointed to Hugh.

'Ough – it's only a bit of fun,' Hugh says.

'Sit down now when I tell you,' he says to Hugh. Then he snapped the glass out of the dim-witted boy's hand and flung the wine into the fire.

'Let the wee fellow enjoy himself,' Hugh says.

'You're a man now,' he says. 'And when I tell you to sit down, I mean it.' The music had stopped. Hugh sat down like a big baby. Bill lifted the bottle of red wine from under Hugh's feet. 'You're drinking no more tonight,' he says.

'Tell me,' Hugh says, 'why are you picking on me?' His big face seemed to droop down more at the corners of his mouth than ever.

'It's for your own good,' Bill says pointing his finger at him. 'You have an old Aunt and she won't last much longer and you're pushing her into the grave.'

'I love her like she was my mother,' Hugh says and his mouth looked almost like crying. 'She'll not die, she'll live for another twenty years yet.'

'I'm telling you,' Bill says. 'You'll not always have her.'

'A'm good to her,' he says and gropes for the bottle, but it was not there.

'Any more trouble from you and you will be out that door,' Bill says and walks away. A lot of the men started talking loud, pretending the quarrel had never happened. After a few minutes the music started again.

Hugh just couldn't keep from houghing and dancing. The dim-witted boy was down on the chair now but Hugh caught his hand and danced around. Suddenly Bill came in and caught hold of Hugh. 'Come on – out,' he shouts. Out.'

'I'm going,' Hugh says; he was like a big soft baby. There was no fight left in him at all.

Then suddenly Ralph sprang out and hit Bill on the side of his face. 'He's doing nobody any harm,' he says, 'let him stay.'

Bill let Hugh go and him and Ralph started into each other. Ralph got him down and held both his shoulders down on the floor. 'Say you'll let him alone,' Ralph says. Bill struggled like the wrestlers on TV do, he was making the same noise too. Hugh was standing against the wall, he was shaking and when he spoke there was a tremble in his voice. The dim-witted boy was watching, he came over and tried to touch Ralph, but someone pulled him away. 'Keep you out of this son,' he says.

'I'm the head of this pub,' Bill was saying. 'And it's up to me who goes and who stays.'

'That's right,' Ralph says and he was still holding him down, both their lips were bleeding. 'That's right,' Ralph says. 'But I don't want you to be picking on an innocent.' Ralph had stopped struggling – he was just sitting across Bill's body holding down his shoulders.

'I want no trouble in this pub,' Bill says. 'I want to stop it before it starts,' his voice was calm now and so was Ralph's.

'I'll see that there's no trouble,' Ralph says.

'That's okay,' Bill says. 'But I'll leave it to you to see that there's no trouble.' The men who were all standing around agreed that there would be no more trouble.

Ralph and Bill got up. When Bill got up Ralph patted the dust from his back and remarked on his cuff-links. Bill told him that they were sixty years old and maybe more if the truth were known.

Hugh sat down in his seat at the fire and there was no more trouble. We drank till well after closing time. When closing time came Maggie put the news on the radio and took the oil-lamp away and put a candle in its place. The light was much dimmer, but the fire kept up a good flame.

When we got home Ma went more than mad. First the boy was sick as soon as he came in the door. We put a basin

down but he wouldn't be sick in it. He would vomit anywhere other than the basin and when we thought he was all
right and let him sit down on the sofa, he was sick all over
his clothes. Ma had to take all his clothes off him and put
Wendy's blue dress on him again.

At first Ma thought the boy was only a bit sick, because
he was that kind of boy, then she smelt Ralph's breath and
there was no holding her. She said that she knew it would
come to this. It would be her son's drinking that would send
her away. She said that she could thank God that Da never
drank. Then she went on and on to Ralph about the type
that went into the pub. She said none of them ever did an
honest day's work in their lives. Ralph said nothing. He just
said if she would have a bit of sense and make a cup of tea.
'You'll be sorry when I'm not here,' Ma says. 'When they
have to bring the ambulance to take me away.'

Ralph says to me. 'Did I hear that silly talk?'

Then when Ma asked me for my pay and I told her that
I had lost it, she cried and bit at her hands like a mad dog.
'For all it was,' I says, 'it wasn't worth bringing home.'

'Open the windows,' Ma says. 'Open the windows and I'll
let the neighbours know what sort of children I have.'
Derek went over and opened one side and he was just about
to open the other side when Ma attacked him with the
brush.

'For God's sake sit down,' Da says. He was watching the
TV; there was a minister on and Da turned it away up loud.
The minister was smiling. 'Jesus said love your brother –
love your fellow men, now this weekend, friends, go out and
sow your seed on good ground. Love your neighbours. Good-
night and may God be with you all.'

Another man came on and smiled and said, 'Good night
and may I remind you to switch off your set.'

Derek was half out the window and Ma was thumping
him on the back with the brush.

'Ma's gone mad and Ralph was drinking,' he shouts loud. Ma left down the brush.

'Come in Derek, please come in and not let us all down.' Derek came in and shut the window.

'Well,' he says, 'is there going to be less noise or will I have to tell the neighbours again.'

'They all know now that my son was in the pub tonight. God forgive me.' She sat down and pushed the hair away from her forehead and closed her eyes. 'Ah well, maybe they'll not always have a mother to break her heart.'

The next morning, Ma went down to the doctor's early. She told him she was suffering from nerves and he gave her a bottle of tranquillizers. It said on the bottle 'take one three times a day', but as soon as she got home she took two.

It said 'keep away from children' and when Derek saw Ma going to sleep as soon as she took them, he wanted to give some to the dim-witted boy, but I said they might kill him. The boy was all right that morning; his clothes were dry and he was none the worse for the drink the night before.

It was Saturday and we didn't have to work. Da was to go to see Aunt Mary that day to see if she would take the boy back. We thought if she didn't take him back soon we would have to go to the police or show her up by writing about her in one of the Sunday papers.

Da didn't get a chance to go, because Ma slept most of the day, after taking the tranquillizers. He had to do the housework and go into the town for the messages. Wendy put on a good dress and we seen no more of her that day. Da said she might as well be out for all the good she was in the house.

Da wrote a letter and sent it with the milkman to Aunt Mary's. It said: 'Dear Aunt Mary. Your son is not much bother. We, me and my wife, feel it would be better if you kept him. He would enjoy living right in the country more. My wife is suffering from nerves and it is a bad time for us to keep him.'

On the Saturday night Ma was still sleeping. Even when Derek emptied cold water on her she still didn't waken right up, the only time she wakened right up was when Wendy came in at night with cow dung all over her dress. She seemed to know that even though she was sleeping. She wakened up quick and ran over and slapped Wendy on the back. Wendy just opened the door slow and walked casually upstairs. Ma went to the bottom of the stairs and shouted: 'Come down here you filthy bitch – if you get into trouble, what's going to happen? Will they marry you? And you only thirteen. The wet's not right dry behind your ears yet. When I was your age I was working in the mill.'

'Things are not the same now,' Wendy shouted down and we could hear her going into her room and closing the door.

Ma went straight asleep after that little outburst and Da had to make the tea. He made fried eggs and sausages; Derek always acted a chap he knew who had something wrong with his tongue and was very fond of sausages; it was said he rode twenty miles one winter's night for a pound of sausages. Derek wouldn't eat sausages himself, because the place where Da got the sausages from had a boy who got his finger taken off with the mincing machine.

On Sunday morning Ma got up as crabbit as hell. The milkman came, but he brought no reply from Aunt Mary. He said when he gave her the note that Da sent, she only laughed; Ma said she would be laughing with the other side of her face before it was all over.

Ralph got up after Ma and Ma told him to take a walk away somewhere out of the road till she made the Sunday dinner. Da got up and got ready for church before he came down for breakfast. Ralph got me up to go for a walk with him. Ma said we better all get up. If we were not going to church, we could get out of our stinking beds and go for a long walk. When Derek got up he wakened the dim-witted boy who was still asleep on the sofa. He shouted into his ear, 'Bang, bang.' That didn't waken him, so he held his nose, but he realized that didn't do any good, because he did all his breathing through his mouth. Derek was going to put his hand across his mouth to stop him from breathing, but his mouth was all wet and so he stuck an old sock into it. That wakened him all right. Ma said now that we had wakened him we could take him out too and not to be going out the front door but to go up the back way where the neighbours couldn't see us in our old clothes. Ralph said that we were going up the back way anyway.

We went a walk nearly every Sunday morning at the top of our back garden. If you could get through the hedge there was a railway line that ran right up close to where we used to live.

Derek and Ralph and the dim-witted boy and me went. It was hard to get the dim-witted boy to go through the hole in the hedge. He wouldn't bend down and when Derek tried pushing his head down for him he cried. In the end we had to force him to bend and push him through.

It was very nice up the railway, there was a very fine drizzle of rain and everything looked clean and fresh. Ralph said that it was funny how we had got used to the dim-witted boy now and it would be odd without him.

The rails were shining like ice and the sleepers were slippery, the telegraph poles at the side hissed with the damp on the wires. The dim-witted boy couldn't walk right on the sleepers. He would take about two steps right then he would be on the stones for a bit. Ralph and I put our arms round him and soon we had him marching out the same as us. Derek said a marching thing: 'I had a good job and I *left* which I had a good *right* to do.' He repeated that until we had walked about half a mile, then we slowed down a bit.

'Let's go up to the old house,' Ralph says.

'Right a'm game,' I say. Derek said we could go if we kept up a steady pace. So we had to smarten up a bit again.

It was a nice walk. On both sides were big high slopes covered in long grass. In the hot days Ralph went up there with no clothes on to sunbathe. Sometimes he took his paints and painted up there. At the bottom just beside the little bridge was a spring; it was good water, Ralph said, better than you could get down in the village. Watercress grew there and Ralph sometimes brought a bunch home. In the summer, if you got a dandelion and pulled the top off you could suck water up through it.

We crossed the gates and continued on up the railway; further up, we came to other gates. They were the gates Alfie Rock used to come out onto the main road; one day he was half across in his car and it stopped. The train was coming, but he didn't get out in time – the care was smashed into pulp and so was he. Two days later they found his head lying behind a ditch two fields away.

Past those gates there were little hilly fields full of winds. There were lots of rabbits; we saw a little black one. Derek said that it was unlucky to shoot a black rabbit. Ralph said that he thought it was a sin to shoot any colour rabbit. Over across the little hilly field was a row of white houses; when I was very young I kept bunnies and a boy who lived in one of those houses went to the same school as me. I told him about the lovely white bunny I had and he said if I could bring it to his house that night he would give me five bob for it. I took it along and sure enough he gave me five bob. It was nice to feel the money in my pocket, but when I was half way down the lane, his mother came down after me and took the five bob back and give me the bunny. It was snowing and it was a fair walk home; before I reached home it had died. Da said that it died through starvation but that wasn't true, because I could feel the corn sliding about in its crop bag. We buried it the next day, Ralph and me, we dug a little square hole and put it down slowly in a shoe-box.

The dim-witted boy was starting to lag behind when we got up to the old house. You could see it just straight across the field from the railway. Ralph had a thoughtful expression on his face when he saw it. Most of the windows were nailed up with corrugated iron. It looked as if it had sunk into the ground with the long weeds and grass growing right up to the door. We went down into it and Ralph stood at the door.

'Boys, oh dear, would you credit it,' he said, 'at one time this was our home.' It was very silent except for the noise of the river down at the back. There was a strong smell of nettles and grass, the wire that Da had put up out at the front wasn't there any more. It had been trampled down by cows or something. Da put the wire up to grow a crawling flower up through it. It grew all right – very fast, little red flowers, but Da had to cut it away because it attracted swarms of bees and it was too near the door. Wendy was only four then and she was always trying to catch them and getting stung: she was a slow learner because no matter how many times she got stung she still wanted to catch them.

Inside Ralph just looked and said nothing. Derek thought it was funny because the big bucket that we used to pee in at night before we went to bed was still there, only it was rusted. A couple of feet up the wall was black now. Derek said that was because we missed the bucket sometimes, the stove was rusted too and the chimney-pipe wasn't there at all. Beside the stove Da had painted the bits of the wall that were sticking out yellow, then he had cut a potato in half and carved out the middle leaving just an uneven circle to dip in the paint and stamp all over the wall to make a design; in some of the circles Derek had scored little funny eyes and a nose and a great big grinning mouth. The circle had almost faded away but you could still see the funny little faces. One of the cows must have got in through the little door because there was cow dung on the floor and the dim-witted boy was standing in it.

I got a very lonely feeling. You could hear the fine rain coming down the chimney. There was nothing there, just silent fields and a deep black water at the back. I was frightened of the distant fields, everything so big and so far away – no end to the sky. Sometimes I used to dream at night about the sky; my body would grow bigger and bigger – getting more and more numb and changing into the colour of stone – then I would think I could feel the sky – feel the air in my fat hands; at first it was good and a real feeling but then my body would continue to get bigger and bigger until I became the earth and that would frighten me so much, because I could only feel like brown-grey clay. I would waken up sweating and my hands would be asleep.

The river frightened me too. After Da took me to see the mad horse getting shot, the day Ma was making raspberry jam, I kept dreaming that I was in the muddy water and there were lots of little horses in the water trying to get at me to bite me and I couldn't see them through the dirty water. I could only feel them touch my naked body with their fleshy lips.

'Come on,' I say. 'We might as well go. We have seen all there is to see.'

'It makes you sad to see this lovely little house in ruins,' Ralph says. 'We all could have been happy here, if Ma hadn't kept on until we had a new house.'

'Sure the thing might have come down round us if we hadn't got out,' Derek says and kicks an old board that had fallen down from the ceiling.

Ralph said we might as well go down to the weir and

have a look at the old place where we used to bathe on Sunday mornings.

The cave was completely grown over with grass. Down at the bottom of the lane there used to be a tiny little stream running under the lane, but there it had sunken down and the water in one side had damned up and was swamping the field; although the field in wet weather was very boggy, there was one part that had a skin of rushes and grass growing over it. They said if you broke through that you would never come out again, it was just bottomless mud. One day two of Jim Hunt's cows sank in there. He had the two cows tied together by the legs, that was to keep them from going over fences. Da said he was bloody lazy that he wouldn't repair the holes in the fences. He thought it was easier to tie their legs together so that they couldn't take wide steps. One day Ralph went and cut the rope.

Ma saw the heads of the cows sticking out of the swamp. They were making a terrible noise. She and Mrs Anderson got a rope no thicker than a piece of string to try and pull them out, but they couldn't even get over far enough to put the rope round them, they were too frightened of sinking themselves. Jim Hunt had to come with the tractor to try and drag them out. He got over to them all right and he was able to get the rope round their necks, but he was a vile-tempered man. He just revved up the big tractor and drove straight forward. You couldn't hear the cows getting strangled for the noise of the tractor. In the end the rope broke and he just drove straight home. Not even stopping to thank Ma and Mrs Anderson for going and telling him.

'Do you remember the time the cows sank in there?' I say.

'It had no need to happen,' Ralph says.

'It couldn't be helped, once they were in there,' I say.

'Their legs never should have been tied,' Ralph says.

'That was to keep them from jumping fences,' Derek says.

'I never heard anybody that could talk nonsense like you,' Ralph says and he was irritated and walking faster.

There was a little path just before we came to the weir, that led down to the spring. To please Ralph we had to go down in there; we drank the water, Ralph and me, but Derek wouldn't drink it because about a month before we left the old house we found a dead rat lying in the bottom, we had to put lime in the spring to purify the water. Since then Derek wouldn't take a mouthful, even with all the forcing Ralph did to try and get him to take it. 'Look at the freshness and the clearness of the water,' he says. 'Look at the soft green moss growing over the stones and it's running fresh all the time. You could never get pure water like that coming through the taps.'

'I don't care if it is perfume,' Derek says. 'I wouldn't touch it. Come on you lot, we better get going.'

We went down along the side of the little river that led right down to the weir. Ralph and me and the boy were in front. Derek had stopped to break a stick out of the hedge. Suddenly he slipped up on us quick.

'Come here quick,' he whispers.

'What?' Ralph says.

'Come now,' Derek says, 'before it's too late.' He was whispering loud and breathing hard.

'What are you on about?' I says. 'If we get to go and have a look at this water flowing over stones, we are already late to go home.' Derek was holding his hand over his mouth to keep himself from laughing loud. His face was red and his eyes were half closed.

'All right,' Ralph says. 'We'll go back to see what you're on about.'

'Hurry up,' Derek says. 'We might be too late, She might have finished.' When we got up to a dense part in the hedge Derek signalled for us to stay down. We crawled up to where we could see through the hedge. Derek was in front.

'You're okay,' he says. 'You're in time.'

'I see nothing,' Ralph says.

'Over there beside that big bush,' Derek whispers.

'Oh God Almighty, I see her,' Ralph says. I crawled up a bit closer and saw her too. It was Mrs Kerr, she was haunched down under the big bush with her elbows resting on her knees and her chin resting on her hands.

'I thought she got a new toilet in,' Ralph says.

'She did,' Derek says. 'But she can't handle it right, she can't get used to it.' The dim-witted boy was watching too and Ralph pulled some twigs down in front of him in case Mrs Kerr would see him. Derek put his hand over his eyes and shook his head slow from side to side and laughed silently. The sketch of Mrs Kerr sitting there, them big bare knees and her thin red spotted face, with hair hanging down both sides of her head like wet string. Ralph settled down and lay on his belly. Derek dug into the ground with his strong hands and cut out a big heavy sod, the clay crumbling from it. He drew back his hand ready to throw it.

'Let her sit — let her sit,' Ralph says.

'If you were behind her you could get her on the bare arse,' Derek says.

'Stay where you are,' I say. 'She might see you moving.' She was looking in our direction, but she didn't see us. Derek sneaked away and the next thing we seen he was slipping up the other side of the hedge. Then we saw him stop just behind her. Once she looked round slow and we thought she might have heard him, but she turned her face back round in our direction.

'I told him to let her sit,' Ralph says.

'She's sitting a long time,' I say. Then Derek thuds her on the arse with the big sod, I never seen anybody get up so quick. She was up and her dress was down, but her knickers were hanging round her ankles. We were all laughing, even the boy. Derek was laughing so loud you could have heard him in the village. She went to run taking little short steps because her knickers wouldn't let her take long ones. Then one leg of her knickers came off and over her shoe and she stopped and pulled them off completely and ran as fast as hell out through the gap in the hedge and up the side of the next field.

'Shit,' Ralph shouts. 'You scored her.' Derek couldn't answer for laughing. He come out through the hedge to where Mrs Kerr had been sitting and pointed to the ground and laughed, bending right back with his mouth open and then forward, staggering.

We went over and there were three little brownish-black looking balls lying there. One had fallen almost on top of another.

'That's terrible,' I say. 'And her a Christian.' This made Derek laugh more than ever.

'If them had been shot out with a bit of air behind them, it would have cracked like a machine gun,' Ralph says. That sent Derek hysterical. He crowed until no noise came out at all and fell onto the grass and vibrated. Ralph and I were trying to control ourselves, but we went to pieces with laughter when the dim-witted boy went over and stuck a thin stick through one of the balls. I thought I was going to die, I couldn't stop and the tears were running out of my eyes. Just when I thought I was going to stop I looked up and the boy was sticking the stick into another ball. I threw myself on the ground too and felt my whole body jerking.

Ralph made the boy throw the stick away and we walked down towards the weir. Every time I thought about it I would burst into another fit of laughing. Derek wouldn't stop talking about it. He said to the dim-witted boy that that was what he was having for dinner. Ralph was always the one for trying to get a tan in the sun and Derek says rub that stuff on and you'll need no sun. He said you could polish your shoes with it too and that's what colours ginger cake.

'Give over now,' Ralph says, 'or we won't be able to eat for a week.'

The dim-witted boy went on in front a bit. We had already crossed the little flood gates that banked up the water, just letting out at night to run the mill wheel and give electric light to three little houses. The river branched off further up and came together further down making a kind of island.

Derek was laughing at the boy because he was walking fast and looking very funny.

'Where's he going to, hurrying like that?' I say.

'Maybe he wants to get up that height to watch that big log coming down the river,' Ralph says.

'It's almost a tree,' I say. 'If you got it out it would make good firewood.'

'It would burn like paper in our stove,' Derek says.

'What's he doing?' Ralph says. The boy was clambering up the little slope by the river. We stopped and watched him. He was almost on his hands and knees, pulling himself up by the thick grass and his face still looking at the sky. All of a sudden he kind of straightened himself up and in a clumsy way just threw himself into the river.

'I could have told you,' Derek says.

'You should have said before he done it,' I say.

'The main thing is to get him out,' Ralph says.

'He deserves to stay there and drown,' Derek says. 'That's what he needs to teach him a lesson.'

'Stop arse fandering about,' Ralph says. 'And come on till we get him out.' He started moving up the slope in front of us fast. Derek went slower.

'I don't give a fiddler's fuck, if he drowns,' he says.

'You can't let anybody drown, not even a dog,' I say.

'He's no wiser than a dog,' Derek says. Ralph was up on the top of the slope. He looks down at us.

'He's not there,' he shouts.

'Maybe he has sunk,' I say. 'You better look hard.'

'That log's over the weir now,' Derek says.

'What?' Ralph says.

'It's over the weir now,' Derek shouts.

'What did he say,' Ralph shouts.

'You didn't say who said what,' Derek says.

'You better look hard,' I say. 'That's what I said.'

'You said something before that,' Derek says and he stood there his face twisted up.

'What did he say when?' Derek says. Ralph always wanted to know what you said there a while ago, even if it didn't matter and Derek always kept him going about that.

He was laughing. 'What did he say when?' he says.

'He must have sunk,' I say. 'That's what I said.'

'I thought you said something else,' Ralph says.

'What else,' Derek teased.

'Shut your mouth,' I say. Ralph was lying down on his belly on the wet grass looking down in. It was about seven or eight feet down into the water. It was a straight stone wall down, with a couple of bushes growing out. The wall curved round one way towards the weir and the other way towards the floodgates and got lower as it went down.

'If he's not down there, he could have gone any way,' Derek says, in a tone that showed he couldn't care less.

'If you don't want to bother, go on home,' Ralph says.

'What the hell would happen if Ma was here now? They would have to come and take her away.' Derek says. Ralph is still lying on his belly. He signalled to me to go further down towards the weir to look.

'He should float,' I say. 'When we all fell into the water at River Side, we came up again.'

'That idiot's not coming up in a hurry,' Derek says. 'Maybe he wants to stay there.'

'Maybe he's dead by this time,' I say. Then I hear a spluttering and coughing. Ralph gets up quick.

'He's still okay – he's round there.' I look down in and see just a head. Ralph comes over.

'I wouldn't jump into that river today to save the Lord Himself,' Derek says. Ralph and me both lie down on our bellies. The head was bobbing up and down. It bobbed up high and Ralph grabbed for it. He caught hold of his hair.

'Keep a hold,' I shout and try to stretch down to get hold of his shoulders.

'Try pulling him up a couple of inches,' I say. Ralph pulls up a bit and I nearly get him, but his hair comes out and he sinks down in again. The wet hair sticks to Ralph's fingers.

'You hold my legs and I'll try stretching down further,' Ralph says. I get up quick and get hold of his legs. He eases forward till half his body is over the edge. I hold his legs hard down on the ground.

'What's he doing?' I say to Derek.

'He's got a good hold on him now,' Derek says. Derek gets down and almost drags the boy out with one hand. He holds him right out of the water.

'You're a silly gornical,' he says to the boy. The boy was like a scarecrow. His glasses had fallen down his face but the National Health wire on them still curved around his ears.

'You're a stupid bastard,' Derek says to the boy, and shook him. 'For two pins I would throw you back in and hold you under.'

'He can't help it,' Ralph says. 'It's something in him that we don't know.'

'That's right,' Derek says. 'Madness, pure madness.' He

drags him onto the little slope and lets him fall like an old, dirty dishcloth.

'We don't know about these things,' Ralph says. The boy was making vomiting noises heaving up little spouts of water. Derek stood close to the boy and looked at him. He twisted his face, as if he were going to be sick, too.

'Boys like that ought to be put down,' he said. Then he moved away and said to Ralph in a very serious voice, 'Should we throw him back in again?'

'Shut up,' Ralph says.

'He doesn't belong to us,' I say. 'Who are we to say what?'

Ralph was sitting on a stone looking at the ground and then at the boy. Water was still coming out of his mouth and you could hear him breathing through the fine drizzle of rain. Derek didn't look at the boy now at all. He stood up with his hands in his pockets, biting at a little slip of rough skin in the inside of his lip. He didn't look at Ralph or me either; he looked at the fine rain falling on the water.

'Who does he belong to?' he says. 'Does his Da want him?' Nobody replied. Then he said louder, 'Does Aunt Mary want him?'

'It doesn't look like it,' I say. 'She would have come back for him.'

'It's true,' Ralph says. 'But there might be a purpose for him being born.'

'Purpose my arse,' Derek says. 'Well if we throw him back in there, they can send another purpose.'

'If you could just forget about it Derek, and shut up,' I say.

'Ma doesn't want him – nobody wants him and he's no good to man or beast,' Derek says, all excited, and goes over toward the boy. There is a little whitish coloured vomit coming out of his mouth now and running slowly down onto his wet coat. Derek pulls him up by his jacket and moves in the direction of the river.

'Let him be,' I say, 'it's not for us to do anything but take him home.' Derek's face was red.

Ralph got up and caught Derek. 'Take it easy,' he says, 'you might be sorry.'

'I'll kill him cold-bloodedly,' Derek says and he looks as if he is going mad. 'I'll kill him – kill, kill.'

'Take it easy,' Ralph says. 'I understand.' Then Derek put both his arms over his face and burst into tears.

'I don't know, I don't know nothing,' he says through the crying. Ralph and me get him to sit down. He was crying hard and there were a lot of tears coming out – I could feel them on my hand, wet and tepid. But I didn't want to take it away from around him, in case he might feel I didn't like him.

'It's not the end of the world,' I say, 'and Ma's having soup for dinner.'

He is crying in quick jerks. Ralph just kept rubbing his shoulders and saying, soft : 'There now, there now.'

'I tried to kill him,' Derek says.

'You were only saying that,' I say.

'No,' he says, 'I meant it.'

'We all feel like this at times,' Ralph says. 'It's like a big basket of apples and two or three with rotten bits in them. We want to throw them out – maybe we do – but maybe we cut out the rotten bits and eat the rest; or like an old egg-bound hen sitting down to die and the other hens pecking at it to make it die quicker.'

Derek blew his nose. His eyes were red and his face was grey and he was shivering. He got up and walked slowly down toward the floodgates.

'You see that?' Ralph says. 'You would think he is as hard as nails, but inside he is just a boob.'

The boy was shivering now.

'He must have taken in a lot of water,' I say.

'If we turn him over on his belly and press on his back, that's how we could get it out of him,' Ralph says.

We turn him over. 'You better do it,' I say. 'I don't know anything about these things.'

Ralph straddled his legs over those of the boy. 'I'm not too sure either,' he says. Then he presses him hard on the waist with both hands – pressing hard up into his body. He keeps doing it. The boy doesn't do anything at first; then he lets out a loud belch and some dirty water splutters out onto the grass.

Derek is sitting down on the floodgates waiting for us to come up.

'We'll be there in a minute,' I shout. Ralph presses the boy up and down for a while more, but nothing comes up. The boy continues to shiver.

'We better get him back fast,' I say.

We got back onto the railway and walked fast. Derek was going a long way in front because two or three times the boy had to stop to vomit, and he kept walking on ahead.

He was already in and had told them all about what had happened. Da came out and stood at the back door watching us come down the garden. He was still in his church dress – a charcoal suit and a red tie. In the middle of the tie was a little white tower and below that it said TS. Da never went to the Tower School, he said he just liked the look of the tie. He didn't have any cuff-links, but when he got the new shirt there were black plastic studs in the cuffs that Da said looked exactly like cuff-links. They had a golden M on them, and he said if his name had been Malcolm or Morris they would have just been made for him.

'Is the dinner ready yet?' Ralph shouts from halfway up the garden.

'What the hell,' Da says. 'Do you want your Ma to come and meet you with it?'

Ma was in the scullery at the window. 'Language,' she says in a jovial voice to Da. 'Watch the language on a Sunday' – she was irritated at Da saying 'what the hell'. You could tell that by the way she spoke. Then she started singing 'The Lord's my Shepherd'.

'This boy will need something warm in him after what has happened,' Ralph says.

'That boy might not be the same boy tomorrow as he is today,' Da says in a casual way.

'What are you on about?' Ralph says.

'What I say,' Da says.

'It doesn't make sense,' Ralph says.

'Faith could move mountains,' Da says.

'I don't see many mountains moving,' Ralph says. 'What are you on about?'

'The boy,' Da says. 'I'm going to take him to be faith-healed.'

'What good's that going to do him?' Ralph says. We went into the kitchen and Da followed us. Derek was sitting throwing a little round cushion up against the ceiling.

'You're knocking the paint off,' Da says. Derek didn't pay any attention to him – he kept on throwing it up, the thin white paint flaking off and falling on his head.

'Do you hear what Da's got into his head now?' he says to Ralph – not paying any attention to Da as if he wasn't in the room.

'This faith-healing lark,' Ralph says.

'Faith could move mountains,' Da says.

'Nonsense,' Derek says, having Da on. 'You got it all wrong – you mean bulldozers.'

'Jasus walked on the water,' Da says looking all serious.

'He'll not do it now,' Derek says.

'Why not?' Da says.

'Because he's got holes in his feet now,' Derek says, and throws himself right back on the chair and thumps the cushion hard against the ceiling.

'Where's Wendy?' Ralph shouts to Ma in the scullery.

'She's still in her lazy stinken bed. You would think a girl who's nearly fourteen now could get up and dry a cup. But no. She would lie there if the house was burning round her,' Ma shouts in. The dim-witted boy was sitting in front of the fire, and the steam was rising from his clothes. Ma came and looked in. 'You'll need to take them clothes off that boy,' she says.

'He'll have to put on Wendy's dress,' Ralph says.

'If you get them off then I'll have time to dry and iron them for the mission tonight,' she says.

'What's all this about?' Ralph asks. He starts taking the boy's clothes off.

'Ask your Da to explain it,' she says.

'What's the use?' Da says. 'He never listens.'

'I am listening,' Ralph says. 'You start the thing in the middle.'

'You never bloody listen,' Da says. 'One's busy telling you something interesting, and you go and pick up a book or comic and start reading.' The TV was on, but the sound was off because Ma said that it wasn't right to put it on on a Sunday. Da had his eyes on it, and was talking to Ralph at the same time.

'You're not listening now,' Ralph says. 'You're watching that thing.'

'There's no sound,' Da says.

'You might as well forget about it, Ralph,' Derek says. 'It's just this fool notion Da's got about getting this idiot cured.'

'He's going to be faith-healed,' Da says. 'There's a man coming to the village tonight that can cure anybody.'

'Who got you onto this lark?' Ralph says. The boy was

standing naked now. His skin was a blue-white colour all over except for round his waist where there was red marks that his tight belt had left. His stomach and chest were the wrong way round – his chest sank in and his stomach stuck out. Even if you could only see his feet you could tell that he was dim-witted. They were long and thin, and his toes came half way along his feet instead of just being open on the end like other people's. There was wide gaps between them too, and big round joints. His little penis looked exactly like a mushroom – and the same colour too.

Derek threw the cushion and hit him on the belly. But he couldn't see who done it because Ralph was trying to get the dress over his head.

'You should dry him first,' Da says. His head was much bigger than Wendy's, and it took Ralph a long time to get it on. When suddenly his head appeared his glasses were not on him. I was surprised his eyes were so small. They were sunk well in, and it looked as if he had no eyelids. Then I saw his eyelids come down. They were red like the skin inside your mouth.

'Put them glasses on quick,' Derek says. The dress was puckered up under his arms, and Ralph fumbled at it for the glasses – suddenly they fell with a sharp crack on the tiles that were round the stove. One glass had broken completely. Ma came in, and she said that he couldn't go to the mission hall like that. Derek said that it would be better to take the other glass out, but Da said that it would be better being able to see with one eye than none. He got some Sellotape and stuck it on but it was a mess: even Da himself thought it would be no good to go to the mission hall with.

In the end it was settled – it was Ma's idea. She had a pair of pink glasses she got six years ago, and they were as good as new – she only wore them for one week until Da bought her a family Bible with bigger print in it. She went upstairs and got them. They were much too wide for the boy, and they kept sliding down his nose. It wasn't that Ma's head was bigger, it was that she got them much cheaper because they were already made, and she just held them on for all the time she used them. When the boy tried to look at anything through them he turned his head in a circle. It was hard for him to walk with them on, and he couldn't find the door handle. Da said that it was just the change, and he would be all right when he got used to them.

Wendy came down and lay on the sofa. She still had a nightdress on. It was a dark blue colour. Ma got her it because she said it was easier to keep clean than a white one. One side was all wrinkled up, and the other side was smooth and shiny – like she had laid on the one side all night. She smelt like the bedroom. That stuffy sleepy smell that seems to cling all over your body in the morning.

'Is the breakfast ready?' she shouts into Ma.

Ma came running out of the scullery. 'Breakfast my arse,' she says. 'There's not another girl in the whole housing estate stays in their bed like you. You should see those lovely girls going down to Sunday School with their nice clean faces and white slippers, and their nice little hymn books in their hands. God, did I ever think I would rear a daughter who can hardly be bothered to clean her own backside.'

'It's as clean as yours,' Wendy says. Her voice is thick like the noise the coal makes when you are trying to break the burnt mass with the poke.

Ma has a spoon in her hand. There is green leeks sticking to it, and soup dropping off. She jumps at Wendy and slaps her feet on the floor like a duck, grinding her teeth like she might eat her.

'Your Aunt Mary was the same,' she says. 'She talked back to her mother – but she's suffering for it now. God knows how to punish the lazy. There's a bath up there – it's where I never seen you in it.'

'Is the dinner ready?' Ralph says.

'I'm talking, I'm talking,' Ma says. 'Somebody's got to talk to this girl.' Wendy picks up a woman's magazine and ignores Ma – as if she is reading hard and Ma's not there.

'You might as well go in and get the dinner out, Ralph,' says Ma, pushes Wendy's legs down from the sofa, and goes back into the scullery.

'This is ready,' she shouts in. Nobody moves and she shouts again.

'We heard you the first time,' Derek says. When we go in there's nothing on the table.

'I thought you said it was ready,' Ralph says. He is annoyed because he is hungry. 'I might as well go back in and sit down till it's ready,' he says, and turns to go back.

'It's nice to have a nice pleasant family,' Ma says, smiling. 'They all look like butter wouldn't melt in their mouth when they're outside, but when they're in the house the devil couldn't look at them.'

In the end we all get round the table. Ma says she hasn't time to eat – she says that after spending all morning cooking, and Wendy lying in bed she doesn't feel like eating.

In the end we have to put the old glasses with one glass in them on the boy so that he can sup his soup without missing his mouth. Derek lifts his plate and takes it into the other room to eat when he sees the boy's eyelid through the empty frame. After dinner he has to put on Ma's glasses again because the chap that Da was speaking to at church, who told him all about the faith-healing man, is coming to see the boy.

When he comes to the door Da and him shakes hands, and then he comes on in. He has a little yellow Austin Seven parked outside with a poster of the faith-healer on it. He shakes hands with all of us, and the dim-witted boy too, and says how nice it is to meet the dim-witted boy. He says he can't stop long because he has to dash off to hospital to see an old woman before she dies. The old woman was ninety and loved God. Da said he admired people like that, and he said that he loved poor people and sick people – he said it done you good to see them sometimes. He was only the same age as Ralph, but Da called him Mr Turner.

'Call me Andy,' he says.

'Call me Bill, Andy,' Da says. He was a little fellow with brown hair well parted and combed down. He wore a brown coat with a belt on it, but the belt didn't make any difference to it – it just went straight down.

'Andy will take a cup of tea,' Da says to Ma.

'No, no thanks all the same,' he says. 'People are kind but I haven't the time.' Ma went into the scullery to make him the tea out of kindness whether he wanted it or not. She signalled for us to come into the scullery. When she got us in she closed the door.

'Do you see that fellow?' she whispers. 'Do you see how clean and tidy he is?' She had made sandwiches out of sliced bread, and cut the crusts off for him.

'What's wrong, has he got no teeth?' Derek says aloud, and Ma caught his arm and nipped it to make him keep his voice down. She had a cream cake for him too, and when she looked round Ralph had taken a bite out of it. She just turned round and shoved him against the wall.

'Cut it out Ma,' he shouts. 'I didn't know it was for him.'

She opened the door and says to Da smiling, 'Are you going to have a cup of tea, Daddie?'

'Daddie, Daddie, Diddie,' Derek sniggered.

'These boys of mine are full of fun,' she says to Andy. 'If they were lying in an iron lung it would be worse – I say as long as they can have fun they're all right.'

'I know what you mean, Mrs Oliver,' Andy says. She had to cut the bit off the cream cake and give him the other bit. Da didn't have any tea – she warned him before Andy came to say he didn't want any because she only had the one cream cake.

'I'm not a big tea drinker myself,' Da says, and Andy said that he heard that too much tea gives you cancer. Da said he could believe it. Andy didn't eat the sandwiches, he only ate the cream cake. Ralph and Derek and me sat and watched him eating it. Derek made remarks to Ma about it, and made Andy blush, and find it hard to swallow.

'You get one of them cream cakes free with every corset you buy,' Derek says. 'They get the cream out of boils on cow's tits.'

Ma says it was really nice to see how many young people went to church nowadays. Derek said that half the village was churches. It was hard to miss going into one. Where they got all the different Gods from he didn't know, because they all preached different things – there was that drinking lot, and the holy rollers and ... 'There's only the one God,' Ma says. 'The Lord Jasus Christ our Saviour.' She said it because she had to stop Derek from letting her down. Andy said there was no getting away from it – we are all God's children.

'He must get a big family allowance,' Derek says, and snorts a laugh and a snot snerts out of his nostrils.

'God loves us all the same,' Andy says. He heard what Derek said and didn't know what to answer. Da said it was nice that he cared for every hair on our head and every grain of sand.

Andy told us that God was the breath of life, and he could work through the faith-healer's hands and cure anything. He said that sometimes there was magnetic oil come through the faith-healer's finger-tips.

Ma said that money could buy a refrigerator, but it couldn't buy faith. That Daddie and her were married nearly thirty years, and money couldn't buy that. I couldn't stop sniggering, and Ma kept looking at me, and I pretended that Derek had stuck his finger in my waist and tickled me. Andy said that he loved everybody black or white or whether they worked in an office or were murderers. He loved them all because Jasus did. Derek said that Jasus drank wine with the Inland Revenue, and Ralph's face went blood red trying to hold in a laugh – in the end he had to get up quick and run out into the hall.

Andy shook hands with us all again before he left. Then he brought out something for the dim-witted boy. It was a photo of Christ in a garden with lots of flowers and plum trees – he was stooped nearly double, and there was blood dropping from him. The photo was held to the glass with a nice little rim of Sellotape. On the picture it said 'Christ died for you'. The boy couldn't see it with Ma's glasses on, and he had to wait till Andy had gone before he could look at it. After he had pulled the Sellotape off he went in and stuck it into some old dish water that Ma had still left in the basin.

Andy said that after he had seen the old woman in the hospital he would call and take Ma and Da and the dim-witted boy to the Faith Mission Hall. Da and Ma said there was nothing that they wouldn't do for the boy now – he was like their own son.

Derek talked nonsense all afternoon. He made the dim-witted boy sit on his knees, and said things to the boy that made Ma cry. 'God let off a bomb and blew the balls off a fly,' he said. 'Jasus was a heavy weight boxer and wore false teeth.' The boy just looked at the fire, and then put his head round and round like a blind donkey. 'The only way to know God is to flush yourself down the toilet,' he told him. Da said that Derek neded curing too – he needed his head looking at.

'No I'm not mad,' he says and gave two or three big in-sane laughs to keep Da going. He stuck clothes pegs onto the lobes of the boy's ears and jumped up and down like a child – 'We re all going to be cured, we're all going to the Faith Mission.'

When Ma told Wendy to go up and change before Andy came, she just went to bed. We went up into her room – Derek fooled around and put lipstick on and perfume.

We decided to go to the Faith Mission – Ralph and Derek and me – to see what it was like. Ma didn't want us to go. She said we would let her down a bagful. She put on a black coat and black hat, and powder as white as flour and red lipstick. Her face looked like a snowman's face with a blob of blood for a mouth.

'How do I look?' she asks Da. He said that it was silly asking him, it was her that was dressing. Ralph said that the lipstick looked ridiculous – that colour wasn't the fashion any more. She put on perfume that you got free if you bought six bars of soap and a shampoo. Ralph didn't like lipstick or perfume. He said that lipstick was made from dead hen's guts, and perfume was made by putting two animals in cages beside each other, and when they were on heat and wanted to get into each other they collected the sweat that they produced.

Da sat in the front of the car beside Andy, and Ma and the dim-witted boy sat at the back. She didn't care who seen her with the dim-witted boy now. She put her hand on his shoulder going out to the car, and earlier on she went into the next-door neighbour's to tell her that if anybody called to see her she would be at the Mission Hall with Aunt Mary's little boy.

We had to walk to the Mission Hall, but we got there just as Ma and Da were going in the door. The Hall had a little yard out in front, and it was crowded with people.

'Let's get in quick and get a good seat,' Derek says. 'Look at that big Bella Duff, if she gets in front of you you'll see nothing.'

'She's built like a battleship,' Ralph sniggered.

As soon as we went through the gate a very well-dressed young fellow came over and shook our hands, and gave us a hymn book each. He said our Mammie and Daddie had just gone in.

'Is this one of these places you roll on the floor,' Derek says. 'I don't want to do no rolling.'

'It's a place where God's children gather together in love,' the fellow says. I felt sorry for him because his mouth went a little bit out of shape with fear and embarrassment.

'Christ died for you,' he snarls. His lips were white and he trembled a bit.

'It's not one of these places they dip you in the water,' Derek says. A big tall man stepped over towards us. He had a long raincoat on with short sleeves, and big hairy wrists. His cap was almost the same colour as his skin and hair, dark, and when he took it off I got the feeling that he had torn part of his real head off. The hair that was under the cap was white, not like the rest of his hair. It must be with wearing that cap, I thought. Because if you move a stone that has been lying on the grass, that bit of the grass will have turned yellow.

'I was baptized in the Great Lake in Canada,' he says, and stood swaying like a long tree, and hitting his leg with his cap.

'What did you go there for?' Ralph says. The young fellow had moved away, and was shaking hands with more people.

'The blood of Christ is everywhere,' he says, and straightened up and looked at us as much as to say, there now think about that : I know a thing or two.

'Maybe the boy should be baptized,' Ralph said to me.

'It looks like he's never done being baptized,' I say.

'You have got to be cleansed in the blood of our Saviour,' the big man said, and opened the Bible in just the right place.

'Jasus will wash your sins away,' he says, and closed the Bible again as much as to say, who could dispute it.

'Fruitie Tutti tore a tit,' Derek says, and led the way into the hall.

Andy was standing at the top of the aisle. He came down and met us, and guided us up into the row behind Ma and Da and the dim-witted boy. You could tell Ma knew we were there, but she didn't look round. Derek put his feet up on the back of her seat, and she eased forward a little bit. Nobody looked anyway, they just sat stiff facing the pulpit. The hall smelt of polish and Brylcreem and new clothes. The dim-witted boy sat between Ma and Da. A bit of his hair stuck up at the back of his head, and Ma turned round and patted it down and smiled at us.

'Do we get tea here?' Derek says, and she turned round quick. There were women sitting at both sides of us now – frightened to move – frightened to breathe too loud.

The first preacher that got up had the pose of a compère on the TV. He was very casual. He had it all under control.

'Friends, let's rejoice in the Lord Jasus Christ tonight,' he says, and smiled – moving his eyes like he was trying to look at everybody individually. He wore a grey suit that had a long jacket. He kept one hand in his pocket all the time, and gestured to us with the other one.

'You can tell he has been watching the goggle box,' Ralph whispers.

'Let Jasus move around us – let his love gather around us,' he says very cool, and stuck his other hand in his pocket – smiling and giving time for his words to sink in. His body was the same shape as an egg with the big end down and his head was exactly the same. He had little round hands too, and his fingers were made up from little eggs of flesh joined together.

'Jasus Christ,' Derek says. 'This meeting's dead.' Ma put her arm round the back of her to nip Derek on the knee to warn him to keep his mouth closed. Her hand groped around, and Derek watched it. Then we started to snigger when Ma nipped the woman that was sitting beside Derek. She was a fiery woman with burning red hair and blood-shot eyes. She was deaf, and sometimes when I was coming home at night she would be standing at the corner shouting at someone who was only a foot away and could hear okay themselves. She never answered the question anyone asked her. Derek said to her one day that he thought it might rain, and she said she was going to buy a horse. One other day Ralph was waiting for a bus, and she was waiting for one too. He said did she think it was running late, and she said it never rained without stopping sometime.

Then the preacher announced that it gave him great pleasure in presenting Jasper Fulton, who would play the saxophone for us. Jasper made his way up the aisle carrying the big case with the saxophone in it.

'This is when they start rolling,' Derek says.

'No, this isn't the Mission Hall that they roll in,' I say. 'They just stick to faith here.'

Jasper got up onto the platform and let everybody see him take the glittering instrument out of its case. He was long and thin, and his face was so closely shaved that it looked as if it had been polished. He stood up and gave two little sharp blows in the instrument. Then he let it hang on his stomach and put up both hands.

'Glory be to the Lord Jasus Christ who died for you,' he shouts.

'It's getting a bit livelier now,' Derek says, and Jasper heard him saying something.

'If anybody has anything to say more than me, let them come up here and say it to everybody, and I'll sit down, but I'm here to rejoice in the gospel – if anybody can think of anything better to do let them do it.' He swung around and clasped his two hands in the air and shouted, 'Everybody join with me playing "What will make you white as snow – nothing but the blood of Jasus – What will make you whole again – nothing but the blood of Jasus. Oh Jasus this I know your blood's as white as snow".' Jasper was swinging. The dim-witted boy had a hymn book, but he didn't look at it. He tried to sit down too, but Ma always pulled him up by the shoulder while she was still singing. Derek thought it was great. He was singing very loud, and holding out the words longer than everybody else. When it came to the end he held the note with Jasper's saxophone for about two or three minutes after we had all stopped. He held up the hymn book like it was a mike, and held out one hand to Jasper to tell him to keep going.

Just after that, without anybody saying anything everybody started singing 'Dropping, dropping, dropping, dropping, hear the pennies fall. Everyone for Jasus he shall have them all.' Da and Andy got up and got two big deep plates. Andy took one row, and Da took the other, and they passed the plates along the lines. They all kept on singing. When Da stood up he pulled a pound out of his pocket and threw it into the plate to start it off.

'Da's mad,' Derek says. 'I never seen him do nothing like that before.' And when he passed the plate down our line Derek took it out. Da didn't know what to do. He made signals for him to put it back, but Derek says, 'I'll give it to you later when you're in your right mind,' and stuck it in his pocket.

After they had collected the plates of money, Jasper said a prayer and played a couple of good going songs. Then another man got up and made a speech.

'I'll not speak long,' he says, 'because we have got a faith-healer who has come twenty miles tonight to show you the power of Jasus. Yes, friends, Jasus has power. He broke the food and fed millions – he made the blind see, the deaf hear, and the lame walk – and friends he raised the dead.'

Derek kept talking all the time. 'It doesn't make sense,' he says. 'If you were dead and went to heaven and somebody brought you back to life. Then you would shoot yourself again to be dead.'

The man shouted really loud now. 'Forget about your TV – forget about your new car. These things are only man-made material things, it's better to follow the spirit of Jasus Christ than to be damned in hell – eternal suffering – hell's damnation. Give your heart to Jasus now, and let him lead the way. Friends he loves you – he died for sinners. Go out and love your neighbour – love the sick and the poor. Let Christ take your hand.'

The faith-healer sprung up from the back like a cat. 'I have no power,' he shouted. 'It's Jasus. Jasus has the power to destroy the world, but he doesn't. Why? Because he loves us all. He has given us power – all of us if only we will use it. Come here – come up here and Jasus will touch you through me if you have faith.' The deaf woman got up and tried to get past Derek's legs, but he kept them up, and she nearly fell trying to step over them. The faith-healer saw her. 'Come here lady, don't be frightened of the power of Christ – he loves you.' The woman went onto the platform, and he grabbed her with both hands. Jasper played the saxophone, and the man shouted 'Jasus has cured. Jasus has touched you.' She stood to the side, and a little woman with a Bible and a battery torch in her hand went up. He did the same thing to her. Then Da got up and took the dim-witted boy, and led him onto the platform. He shook hands with the faith-healer, and left the boy on the platform and sat down again. Jasper played – the sweat was making his face shinier than ever. The healer felt the boy's body all over. Ralph was sitting with a pained expression on his face.

'This'll do him no good,' I say, but Ralph is watching hard. The boy always turns and tries to push the healer's hands away.

'That's doing him no good,' Ralph says, 'he should let him be.' Then the healer takes the boy's head between his hands and holds it. The boy looks as if he is trying to get away.

'He's hurting his head,' Ralph says. Then I can see the boy's crying.

'Let him be,' Ralph shouts, 'he's okay as he is – it's the way he is and it's not up to nobody.' Everybody is looking at Ralph now. He is standing up shouting 'let him go'. The healer is holding the boy's head tight, and his eyes are like a madman's eyes. Ralph clambers out onto the aisle and onto the platform. He catches the boy and pulls at him. The healer is breathing hard, and still holding the boy. Then before I know right what's happening Ma and Da are up trying to pull Ralph off the platform, but Ralph won't let the boy go, and he looks like he's crying too. The boy's face is getting redder, and it looks like the preacher might have his hands round his throat.

'Stop the music,' Derek shouts. They are all making a noise, and I can't tell whether it is singing or shouting. Ma and Da have the hold of one of Ralph's arms, and he has the hold of the boy with the other. Suddenly the healer falls, and Ralph has broke loose from Ma and Da, and pulls the boy quick down the aisle. Ma and Da try to lift the healer up. He gets up and leans against the wall. He is still breathing fast. Ma and Da sit down. The two women who were up to get healed come over towards him again. They moved away when Ralph rushed up. They shake hands with him, and go and sit down. Jasper is playing low now, and when the healer shouts he stops playing altogether.

'The power of Christ is strong,' the healer shouts. 'It is

overpowering spiritual power – it could ruin the world in a second.'

'They can do that anyway,' Derek says.

'Where's Ralph gone?' I say.

Ma and Da go up and thank the healer after the meeting is over, and Derek and I go on home.

We only walk, but we get there as soon as Ma and Da in Andy's car. Da wants him to come in for a cup of tea, but he says thanks all the same – he has a lot to do. Ma looks towards the window. There is no light on in the house.

'Where's Ralph?' I say.

'Whether he's here, or whether he's not here he let me down in front of everybody tonight,' Ma says.

'Maybe he's gone out for a drive with Benjie Glass,' Da says. 'That was his van I seen pull out as we come in.'

'Them boys can get drunk even if it's Sunday or not,' Ma says.

'He's maybe in bed,' I say. 'He was a bit upset anyway.'

'Get in. Get in the gate,' Ma says. 'We'll soon find out. If he comes in drunk with that poor boy he'll not get in.'

When we got in the house looked the same way we left it except when we went upstairs to see if Ralph was in bed. Blankets were missing and his paints and easel and his clothes, and then Ma found the kettle and an oil lamp were missing too. Da said, 'He's gone out of his mind – just when we were getting the boy cured.' Da always thought Ralph was mad because he used to live in the trees with nothing on, and when we moved into the new house and the weather was good he lay up the garden in the sun and took off all his clothes. There were about twenty houses all up our row – all looking down onto our garden. Ma didn't know he was up there naked until the policeman come to the door.

Then she and the policeman had to go up and hold a blanket round him until he put his clothes on again. The policeman said if it happened again he would be taken up for indecent exposure, and Ralph said that didn't make sense – not being able to look at the only body you have got without it being a crime.

'Just when we were doing our best for the boy Ralph goes and does something silly,' Ma says. She says you could do nothing but like the boy after you got used to him. Da said that he would stay off work for a week and get all the faith-healers in the country to look at him. If he had a hundred pounds he would give it to get him cured like it was his own son.

'It's Wendy,' Ma says. 'She's just like your Aunt Mary – filthy bitch – turning people against their own mother, and making them do daft things.'

'What's it got to do with Wendy,' I say.

'It's her,' Ma says. 'She's mixed up in it some way, and I'm saying no more.'

'You don't know anything,' Derek says. Ma closed her lips and tried to say no more like she said she would.

'Wendy's going to have a baby,' Derek says.

'Less of that filthy talk,' Ma shouts.

'Did you ever have a baby?' Derek says.

'It's God makes babies,' Ma says, 'so shut your mouth.'

'I'm having nothing to do with it,' Da says. 'You can never do anything right in this bloody house – no matter what you do for the best.'

'My head's sore,' Ma says. 'There's nothing but worry, worry, worry.'

'If it's not the scab it's the skitter,' Da says. He always said that to Ma when she was complaining.

'If something happens to her,' Ma says, and sits on the sofa and holds her head. Some of the thick white powder on her face has stuck onto her lipstick. Derek sits back on the chair and tries to lift his feet up and touch the wall behind with his toes.

'If anything happened to her I could never show my face out the door, and she would have to go away to England or Dublin,' Ma says.

'She's too young,' Da says, and looks at the silent screen. There was a man and a woman throwing balls through holes. Derek brings his feet down with a loud slap on the floor, and almost falls off the chair. He looks at Ma.

'Sadie, Padie Knicker Neddie – Fon Freddie Bob a Laddie.'

'Shut up that fool nonsense,' Ma says. She was trying to cry. Her face was the right shape, but there were no tears. Da just watched the TV until the minister come on and said to think about your neighbour instead of yourself, and it would be a happy world. Then Da turned it down again and asked Ma if she heard that.

'I knew things were too good to last,' Ma says. 'I felt something was going to happen all day.'

At bedtime neither Ralph nor Wendy nor the boy had come in. Ma was scratching her face and biting her nails. Da said take it easy, there was no point in worrying yet unless we heard she had got killed or drowned. Ma said there was that many bad people around – they might pull her into a car and murder her. Anyway, Da wound up the clock and set it half-an-hour fast to get up early. There was no point in him staying up and worrying if Ma was going to stay up and worry.

Da got into bed, and Ma put the lights out downstairs and locked the doors. She said that if Wendy was out with some man she would never get into the house again. She stood in the bedroom, and every now and then Da told her to have some sense and come away from the window and not have people talking about her, and he couldn't sleep if she was going to stand awake. Derek shouted in for them both to go to sleep, and let Ralph and Wendy stay out if they didn't come in now.

Da was nearly sleeping when a big yellow car pulled up outside – Ma said that was Wendy with a boy. She knew the car, it belonged to a big farmer's son who gave a girl a baby, and the baby was born dead so she never got a penny for it. Da hopped out of bed and pulled on his trousers. He said he would soon put an end to her arsing about with boys. Ma caught hold of him, and told him not to be starting a row out on the street on a Sunday night after him being to the meeting hall. He rushed downstairs and out to the car. He opened the car door, and the boy was lying on top of a girl in the back seat.

'Fuck off,' he said to Da, and Da closed the door and come up in again. He didn't see whether the girl was Wendy or not, but he said it wasn't, but he couldn't get to sleep either after that. About half an hour later the car roared away, and gave the horn a long beep.

Ma must have been busy looking out the front window when Wendy came down the back garden and climbed up in through the scullery window.

It was Derek who said there was somebody downstairs: Da went down first, and Ma followed him in case it was a burglar. Wendy was writing a letter, and Ma tore it out of her hand and read it. It said 'Dear lovely pussy cat I do love you, and I want your baby. There is ...' Ma just drew off and hit her on the mouth.

'I can write another letter easy,' she says as if Ma hadn't hit her at all. Down one side of her dress was cow-dung. Da pulled her up onto her feet, but she still kept her knees bent like she was still sitting. Then he hit her loud on the side of her face.

'Where's the boy and Ralph?' he says.

'What do you ask me that for?' she says, and she was

nearly crying, and inside she wanted to hit Ma and Da. Ma gives her a good shaking.

'Get to bed,' she shouts, and pushed her against a chair. Wendy put her hand up just in time to save her head hitting the corner of the chair, but her hands got it. She threw herself back holding her face with her hands, but she still wasn't crying. Da and Ma had to make her cry before it was finished. Da was wearing just a shirt. His legs were thin and white, and the shirt was wrinkled where it had been tucked between his legs.

'She'll listen to no one. You have no control over her,' Ma says to Da.

Da says 'We'll see,' and he thumped Wendy across the back of the head when her head was down, and when she lifted it up ready to cry, he thumped her on the face. Then she lifted the poker to hit Da back, but she didn't. She threw it right through the window, and started sobbing loud. Ma said that Da shouldn't have hit her on the head – it was dangerous. Da said that he couldn't do anything right. If he did nothing it was wrong, and if he hit her it was wrong too. He said he was going to bed for all the good it would do him because he was past his sleep now.

I was awake most of the night – I heard every car and van going past, but Ralph and the boy didn't come home. I was frightened in case anything had happened to them. I always got the feeling Ralph didn't really want to live, and I would be frightened to be without him. It was just when we moved down into the village – he said it was unnatural. That all them rows of houses just looked like false teeth. Sometimes I got the feeling that he just wanted to be a cow walking in the grass with big sad brown eyes. Just seeing the world in their big heads, and saying nothing. But he couldn't be a cow any more – his brain wasn't right for it. That's why I think he liked the boy, because he was not better than an animal, and he never said nothing.

When I wakened in the morning I could feel his body beside me. I could see his eyes lying awake – wet and sad, and I hugged him in the dark, but when Ma came in and switched on the light he wasn't there.

I had to go to work, but it was hard. Ma and Da wouldn't talk about him. I asked if they thought he might have taken the boy to Aunt Mary's, but Da just said, 'Who knows what?'

I worked with Buster again. Everybody knew about what happened at the faith meeting the night before. There was a rumour going round that Ralph had killed the boy. I knew he hadn't because Ralph wasn't mad in that sort of way – he loved the boy.

At lunch-time Malcolm Harris came up to me. He knew I was worried because in the morning I had to cough when I was riding up to work with him. I coughed, and all of a sudden I started to vomit. He stopped and held my head until I strained a little puke out of the bottom of my stomach.

'Your brother will be all right,' he said. 'Don't worry son.'

I was with Buster when he came up to me and told me that he had heard that Ralph had gone back to our old house in the country, and the boy was living with him. He said he would be okay there. It wasn't far from our old school-teacher's house, and he would help him look after the boy. Ralph and the teacher were very fond of each other – when Ralph was at school him and the teacher used to go for long walks in the country: they liked the same things. After the teacher was supposed to give one of the little girls a bad book about love to read, and after he wrote a book saying that all the teaching in schools was wrong, they made him leave, and the teacher never taught any more. He did painting instead, and made things out of clay too. After that Ralph and he met a lot and it was he who sold some of Ralph's pictures for him. The ones of trees he sold in Ireland, but the ones of naked men and women were sent to England or France.

'They'll be all right up there,' Malcolm assured me, and Buster said too that they would be all right.

After that Buster and I sat and talked for a long time. He was always telling me things that he didn't want other people to know. He brought out an old wallet and showed me a photograph of a girl lying on her back with one knee up.

'I look at this now before I got to sleep,' he says. 'Sometimes if I can get asleep after that I have nice dreams.'

'What have you got in there?' I ask. There was a circle worn in his wallet like something had been there a long time.

'It's to put on,' he says, and blushed and fumbled with his penis in his pocket.

'To put on what?' I say.

'It's rubber – very fine rubber,' he says.

'Looks like a key ring wearing through the leather,' I say. We were sitting under the vats. He looked to make sure there was nobody around, then he brought it out. It was fine rubber like silk rolled into a ring. He undid his fly without speaking, and without looking at me rolled it onto his penis.

'It feels lovely,' he kind of whispered.

I could see Bob Wright's feet coming down the stairs. 'Put it in quick,' I says, 'we should be at that machine now.' He got it in just in time.

'What are you pair playing at?' Bob Wright says. He could see Buster was embarrassed.

'Just chatting,' I say.

'Well chat away up to that machine,' he says. Buster kept his hands in his pockets, and went up the stairs.

'Put a move on or you'll get a kick on the hole,' Bob Wright says. He walked behind us until we got to the machine, then he went away.

'Can I watch the machine while you hank?' Buster says. Then he whispers, 'I want to feel it.' I got up onto the truck, and he started the machine and I did the hanking. I could see him sitting like he was in a dream. I always dreamt too when I was watching the machine – it was the rhythm, and the constant trickling of white cloth falling into the water that made you go like that, and Buster was feeling between his legs too.

Out of the corner of my eye I see old Andrews coming up the floor. I try to let Buster know, but he is just sitting on that box feeling between his legs. I can see his hands moving, and old Andrews can see it too because he is right behind Buster, but I didn't notice the machine was jammed – the cloth was winding round one roller and tearing it into shreds. I shouted and Buster pulled the lever out quick and stopped the machine – but it was too late. There was a lot of cloth ruined. I jumped down from the truck and ran round. Old Andrews was telling Buster to put on his coat and go home to hell, and not come back. Buster was hurt and guilty. He didn't look at me because he was about to cry. He just went and got his coat.

'It could have happened to anybody,' I say.

'I'm not asking for your philosophy,' he snarls and I could see his sharp-looking little teeth.

Bob Wright came hurrying up. 'What's gone wrong here?' he says. 'The trouble is this roller is cracked.'

'Well why wasn't a new one put in?' Andrews said.

'There's one on order, but we can't hold up production until they decide to send it,' Bob Wright says, and looked at me. 'Was it you that was watching the machine?'

'I have sent the chap home who was watching it,' old Andrews says.

'That's one of our best workers,' Bob Wright says, but Andrews didn't pay any attention to him. His old head was quivering with anger.

'Get this sorted out before you go home.' He looked at me. 'I've been wanting to see you in my office – so I will be expecting you.'

It took us the rest of the day to get it off the rollers and sew it up, and get the machine to work again. Then after all that Bob Wright ran the machine himself, and I hanked the cloth onto the truck after the rest of the workers had gone, because the night-shift workers were on short time that week and we couldn't leave the cloth in the vat overnight.

Bob Wright and me got on well together after they had all left. He gave me nice sandwiches that his wife had made for him, and he said that he would bring me in a piece of nice home-baked cake the next day. When we had finished he told me that it would be better if I went and apologized to old Andrews, otherwise he would never be off my back. I said I would, and he put his thumb up and rode off.

When I went to the Old Man's office, I saw him through the window sitting behind a desk talking to Jim Smith. Jim Smith noticed me at the window so I had to go in.

'Here's the boy who breaks windows for no reason,' he says, and looked at old Andrews. 'I'll leave you to him,' he says as if he was leaving the Old Man to give me a good hiding. 'I'll maybe get this little bit of work settled up, and come and show it to you if you haven't already gone,' he says, going out of the door.

The Old Man looked at his pocket watch. 'I should be here a little longer,' he says.

The Old Man sat and stared at me like it was a big strain on the muscles of his yellow eyes – his head quivering.

'I don't know why I broke that window,' I say. 'Something came over me – I wasn't thinking.' His mouth twisted with hatred. His thin dry weathered lips wrinkled.

'You are a very rude boy,' he says, 'and we can't have boys like you here – we want young men with manners that respect the directors.' He leant forward and put a trembling hand on the desk.

'I'll say I'm sorry,' I say. I was frightened he was going to sack me because Ma would never get over that, because everybody would know – and all that trouble with Ralph and the boy. Then I remembered how sorry I felt when I saw poor Buster going to get his coat, and him not even able to say cheerio to me in case he would cry.

'You're just shit,' I shout. 'You're just a man like any other man – but you expect people to crawl to you – you think the sun shines out of your arse.'

'Get out of this factory,' he shouts. It sounded like his voice wasn't catching right.

'Get out, and never come back – that's an order.'

I left the office – I had gone all silent inside – I couldn't see a thought in my mind – my muscles and nerves wouldn't let go. They were tense.

I can't remember riding home – but when I got there Derek met me in the scullery.

'Ma had a bad day's worry today,' he says. 'And she had to go to the doctor again. He said that she might have to go into a mental hospital. I was here at the time – he told her that her trouble was only worry, and not to get upset about it because it was just the same as a bad heart only it was nerves.' I was going on into the kitchen, but he pulled me back – 'They'll have to put her in a straitjacket, and remove part of her brain,' he says.

'Who's in the kitchen?' I say, because I could hear a lot of voices.

'She'll be locked in a padded cell,' he says.

'Stop fooling around,' I says, 'who's in there?'

'Jasus,' he says.

'What do you mean?' I say.

He sniggers. 'It's Aunt Mary in there and her minister, the boy's father – you'll never guess what.'

'What?' I say.

'Ralph has kidnapped the idiot boy and is keeping him in the old house.'

'So what?' I say. 'Ralph knows how to look after him.'

'Not for long,' Derek says. 'Because that's what they're here for tonight – the minister, and Aunt Mary and Da and Ma say that they're going to take the boy and put him in a hospital too – for backward children.'

'He's better where he is,' I say. 'That's what Ralph would say too because he loves the boy – and anyway there's nobody can prove that the boy's the minister's son. So he can't send him away.'

'You just need to go in and look at him to know that,' Derek says.

When I went in Da stood up and told the minister that I was the youngest boy, and had fixed myself up with a job in River Side Factory. The minister shook hands with me, and looked at the ceiling. He was just like a big dim-witted boy.

Aunt Mary and Ma were sitting together. They were very friendly now. Ma didn't look too nervous, but I didn't dare tell her about getting the sack. They were all talking about Ralph. They said that it was the schooling he got. The teacher had him drawing trees and naked bodies before he ever knew how filthy it was. The minister and Da agreed that it would be okay for the ambulance to go and collect the boy tomorrow. Da said that it was best for the boy's sake, and he would take the day off work to see that things would go all right. Ma was talking to Aunt Mary, but she stopped long enough to let her hear what Da had said. Then she said to Aunt Mary that she knew Da, and she knew that he would be up to the hospital every weekend to visit him and take him Lucozade. The minister said that once the boy got settled in with all the other boys he wouldn't be wanting to come home. Ma said that after he got in there for a bit he could come out and do a normal job in River Side Factory like me. She said that I was trying to work my way up. She said that Ralph had got no go in him, all he wanted to do was lie around painting pictures. The minister said that it wasn't for him to judge – it was the Lord, and he was sure the Lord would think that Ralph was a bad influence on the boy – the boy needed to be in an institution where he got scientific and medical attention. Ma started to get nervous again.

'Do you think it'll be safe leaving the boy up in that old house until tomorrow?' she says.

'I'm going up there tonight to see him,' I say.

'Don't talk nonsense,' Ma says, 'it's not safe to go up into the heart of the country in the dark.' Ma really couldn't care a fiddler's fart what I did now, she was too interested in what they were all talking about.

I asked Derek if he wanted to come with me, but no, he said he would observe the situation from down here, and give me a report when I got back.

I got a bit of bread and cheese, and ate it while I was riding the bicycle. I wanted to see Ralph, because he was part of me – we knew each other well, sometimes without even speaking.

I finished the bread and cheese and rode fast. My mind was thinking the same as Ralph's now. I wanted to see him. He could put my mind into words. Our new house was an electric light bulb in my mind, full of the Reverend Marks and Aunt Mary and Ma and Da, and maybe Andy the preacher. But Ralph wasn't in it, nor even Derek nor Wendy;

they were all out of it like me – like we had been cast out of heaven. Because in my mind heaven was an electric light bulb too, and them same people in it and Jasus and maybe God too – or maybe God was the electric light bulb – and getting brighter like the adverts on TV. And Da would get into the TV and talk to Jasus. And Da would try to see Jasus's point of view. But I would be better out of that big clean electric light bulb, like Ralph was.

The road was dark and there was a high bank of trees on both sides. If I was close to the trees, I could smell them and the earth too, and maybe I wanted to eat and be buried in it and smell it all the time. I could smell it now. Because to go to our old house you had to come off the road and into an old rough field.

I could see the light in the old house when I was going up by the river, and that made me feel better. I had to walk because there it was all humps and hollows and too dangerous to ride. I wanted to get there faster than I could. When I counted to ten or to twenty I lost count and I was there. It was like I had never left – like I had never even been in the village, and it looked good.

Ralph was painting an odd picture. It was a woman lying down with nothing on and a tree growing out between her legs, and the apples from the tree were falling into her mouth. The boy was sitting at an old table that we hadn't taken with us to the new house, still with his old glasses on and one glass missing. He was feeling at a photograph in a big book.

I told Ralph about them going to take the boy to a hospital, or a home for that kind of person. He got upset.

'He's staying here,' he says. 'And Master Burney and me are going to teach him things.'

'He's not your son,' I say. 'So I think they can take him.'

'They'll not take him to an institution for eejits. They'll let him be, they'll not take him away.' When he said 'They'll not take him away,' it was like he was going to cry. Then he brightened up and got excited.

'Last night I talked to him, and he understood. He was able to get ready for bed himself. I got a nice bed made up for him – it's warm and he knows it's his.' He looked at the boy sympathetically. 'He just hasn't had a chance, that's all.'

'I think he's better with you,' I say. 'You understand more.'

'He's good company when I'm painting too, he sits and watches me.'

He showed me the boy's bed. It was a little bed with plenty of blankets on it. It was just under the back window. Ralph's bed was by the other window – it was big and fell down into a hollow in the middle and it had hardly any blankets on it. He said that I'd better stay the night instead of riding all that way back down into the village again.

'Ma would worry,' I say.

'She'll worry anyway,' he says. 'It's in her to worry.'

I stayed and he made tea and toast for us before we went to bed. As soon as the boy had finished, he started taking off his clothes and put on one of Ralph's old shirts.

'That's him,' Ralph says proudly. 'He knows a lot now.'

The boy got into his own bed and lay with his glasses on. Ralph and I got into the big bed. I didn't sleep very well – we lay and talked for a long time. Then I realized that Ralph was asleep and I had been talking to myself.

It was very silent after being in the village, except for the constant roar of the river at the back of the house going down over the weir. Once a little branch of a tree fell onto the roof and slid down slow and stuck. Ralph wakened a little bit then, but soon his breathing got deep again. A picture of old Andrews at work came into my mind – his old withered face seemed to be part of my brain, and I never wanted to go back to River Side Factory again. I wanted to stay here with Ralph. Where he knew me and I knew him. I tried to stay awake and think about the things around me, to keep the old weathered face out of my brain. But maybe I was sleeping again, because I thought I saw the boy getting up, but I just lay there. He moved around the dark room for a bit. Then I thought he got back into bed again, but he didn't because when we wakened in the morning his bed was empty. We put on our clothes quick and ran out. The first place we looked was the river. Ralph was shaking and his lip quivered when he spoke.

When we saw him we couldn't tell whether he was already drowned or not, or whether he was swimming. He was right near the floodgates where the water branched four ways – three ways to go through the floodgates and one big branch that went right over the weir like a big sheet of glass, going up into a big white brown curl at the bottom. From where we were, we could see his head looking almost bald with the thin wet hair on it.

'He's moving,' I shout.

'Run,' Ralph shouts. 'Run past him to the floodgates and we'll get him coming down with the current.'

'He's moving down,' I shout.

'He's still alive – he's walking,' Ralph shouts.

'You said he'd come down with the current,' I say.

'I know,' Ralph says. 'But get down stream quick.'

'He's like Jasus walking on the water,' I say. 'Only he's walking under it.'

'I don't believe it,' Ralph shouts. 'Get going.' I ran down stream fast, but I couldn't keep to the side of the river because there was a barbed wire fence there to keep the fishermen from going through our garden. I went up and through where the gate was. When I got down to the floodgates I could see him. His head was out of the water okay, so he wasn't drowned yet – not yet, but it got deeper again before it got shallower near the weir. So if he was going to walk all the way down he would be drowned before he got to me. Ralph was climbing over the fence near to where the boy was.

'It's quicker to go up and through where the gate is,' I shout.

'I'm over now and I don't want to lose sight,' he shouts, and jumps.

'What's his name?' I shout.

'I never knew it, but I call him Herby,' Ralph shouts.

'You shout it – if he comes for that name,' I shout.

'Herby!' Ralph shouts. 'Herby son.' The boy looks up, then his head goes under the water again.

'God almighty,' Ralph says. 'Is he sucked down?'

'No,' I say. 'There's no hole there. He went down with his own accord.'

'He's still got his glasses on,' Ralph shouts.

'You're near now,' I say. 'There's no need to shout.' Suddenly the boy's head comes up again.

'He should be dead now,' I say. 'Remember when Ma said, if you hold your breath for more than two minutes you are dead. He's been under more.'

'He's okay yet,' Ralph says, and he was staring hard at the boy's head in the water.

'Herby son, Herby son,' he shouts.

'It's not true too,' I say.

'What? – Herby son,' Ralph keeps on shouting.

'Jasus,' I say.

'I know,' he says. 'It's impossible.'

'What's that coming down behind him?' I say.

'It's a dead pig,' he says.

'It's coming straight for him – it'll knock him down.'

'It's a dog.'

'No, you were right the first time – it is a pig,' I say. It was a pig. It just missed the boy's head – like it still had a mind of its own – it swung round him slow.

'Did you see that near thing,' I say.

'I seen it all right,' he says. 'It would have knocked him over.'

'It looks like it can still think,' I say. The pig comes down slow and swings round a bit, then it looks like it's stopped. Then it sails quick down into one of the floodgates and sticks. Ralph looks round quick, then back to the boy's head in the water. I never got time to say, 'Don't jump, you can't swim,' before he was in too. We had all been reared beside the water, but none of us could swim. Ma said we would drown. Ralph had a blue shirt on and I could only see it for a time through the water. Then his head came up, like a grown-up child's. His head was covered with hair and his body was hooped – his hands were splashing.

'Do it slow and you'll stay up,' I shout, because that's what Da said. But he didn't hear me. He was splashing faster and he was moving, but he wasn't moving the way his hands were splashing. He was moving towards the weir because the current was strong there.

'I can't jump – I can't save . . .' I was shouting, half-standing and half-crouching – I couldn't. Ralph was mad and splashing, and I was shouting really loud.

'Get out.' I just seen the legs in the grey sky, like a bird, and Master Burney was in the water almost beside Ralph, because he hadn't moved all that far from the side. The master had still got his coat on. It was dark grey now. He grabbed at Ralph, but Ralph went down, and came up quick and grabbed his arms round the teacher and they both went down. When they came up the next time the teacher had broke loose from Ralph and was further away. He swam towards Ralph quick – lifting his arms out of the water and it clinging to him and breathing like it was sticky. Ralph was choking on the water. The teacher brought down one heavy blow and Ralph was still and the teacher's legs were moving slow and he was dragging Ralph with him. They swam further down to where the water was shallower and the bank was low. Then the teacher stopped swimming and stood up: the water was shallower than I thought. He carried Ralph over his shoulders and he looked as if he was dead, but when he put him down on the grass he said, 'Herby son.' The teacher looked up the river and I looked up too, but we couldn't see the boy. Soon Ralph got up and walked onto the little slope again.

'Where is he?' he says.

'Search me,' I say. 'It was you I was looking at: you shouldn't have jumped in.' Then there were little hoops in the water like a fish coming up for a fly. But it wasn't – the hoops got bigger and bigger and the boy's head snorted out of the water.

'Herby son,' Ralph shouts. The teacher was looking hard too.

'He hasn't got any glasses on,' he says.

'This way,' I shout.

'Herby!' Ralph shouts in an hysterical voice and looks like he's going to jump in again, but the teacher pulls him back.

'He is swimming Ralph,' he says. 'But he can't see where he is going.' The boy's head stayed out of the water for a bit, then he ducked under again and you could tell by the top of the water that he was swimming under it.

'Stay here,' the teacher says and went down to where it was shallow and hopped in. He walked slow dragging his legs along. The water was only up above his knees but it got deeper as he went up river. Ralph wasn't looking at him – he was looking at the wrinkles that the boy was making on the surface of the water, that the teacher was walking towards. The boy's head came up again and he was snorting like a horse. He was swimming slow – but not going towards the teacher.

'He doesn't see very much without his glasses on,' Ralph shouts. He was swimming about fifty yards away from the teacher, to his right, going towards the floodgates. The teacher stood up to his neck in the water until the boy came up level to him about twenty feet towards the floodgates.

'Grab him,' I shout. But he didn't: he was saying something to the boy and the boy was swimming towards him now. Then they were both swimming together, and the teacher still talking to him all the time. Before they got to the weir the teacher stood up and the boy stood up too, and we went down to meet them. The boy had only Ralph's red shirt on and the dye was running down his legs.

The teacher said that he thought it would be better if we went back to his house, because he had a fire already lit, and we could get dried out.

Ralph took the boy's hand and we all walked fast.

It was a big house the teacher lived in, and I had never been inside it before. Outside it was all painted white except round the windows where it was painted black. His wife came out to the door to meet us. She looked a bit like the house, with her fat white face and her black friendly eyes. A big black dog came twisting itself down the yard, wagging its tail. It went straight to the boy and sniffed up under his shirt and the boy went closer to Ralph.

'It's all right son, its only being friendly,' Ralph says.

Mrs Burney called, 'Rex,' and it went running to her. She patted it and it curled almost into a circle and licked her white arm.

When we got inside, it kept on licking up under the boy's shirt until the master had to put it into another room.

We sat in the kitchen where there was a big black polished stove. The steam was rising off Ralph and the boy. The Master and his wife went upstairs and we sat silent with our mouths open, and looking around the kitchen. I was looking right round behind me at a big row of blue-rimmed plates when I heard them coming down the stairs and I looked back quick to the fire – as if my eyes had never left that place since they went out of the room. The teacher had on a nice pair of brown corduroy trousers and a big white sweater that I had never seen him wear before. His wife had a big armful of well-ironed clothes. She put them down on a chair and looked at Ralph. 'I will be able to fit you out okay, but I'm not too sure about the boy. You see my sister's young boy comes here sometimes, for the summer months, but his things might be a little too big.' She was lifting the clothes slowly and thoughtfully and looking at the boy – then she lifted them quick. 'Never mind you can try them and no harm done, if they don't fit.' She nodded for Ralph and the boy to follow her. Ralph took the boy by the hand and followed her.

'Don't worry your head about me Mrs Burney,' Ralph was saying.

When they came back they looked new. Ralph had on a nice light pair of trousers and a red sweater. The boy had on a pair of grey trousers that were just a little bit too big, and a white stiff shirt and blazer with a crest on it, a T with an S curled round it in gold. He had new shoes on too.

'Who are those two fellows,' the master says, pretending not to recognize them with their new clothes on. Ralph tried to let his arms hang loose, trying to be at ease. The boy was stiff too – like if he bent his clothes would splinter. He was okay except for his eyes : his eyelids looked like two red scars – like the glasses had been rubbing against them all the time.

'If he had something to cover his eyes, maybe,' I say.

The teacher straightens up and put his hands on his hips. 'We will soon see to that,' he says, looking sideways at his wife.

'Well they'd better get something to eat first,' his wife says and started cooking something.

'Don't bother your head about us,' Ralph says, but Mrs Burney paid no attention to him. He looked a bit puzzled. 'What did you mean?' he says to the teacher. The teacher leaned against the sideboard and tucked his thumbs into the tops of his trousers. Then he put one hand up and pinched the point of his nose, the way he did at school sometimes before he said something.

'I thought we might take Herby into the town today to see an optician,' he says to Ralph.

'That's all right by me,' Ralph says. Then the teacher looked at the boy. 'You would like a new pair of glasses son,' he says. The boy pushed himself against Ralph in a shy way. Ralph looked pleased.

'He's not a bit shy when there's just me and him,' he says.

'Come over here and sit down,' Mrs Burney says. She had left out big plates of fried soda bread and eggs and bacon on the table.

'You shouldn't have bothered about us,' Ralph says, and sits down.

The teacher jerks his head towards the table. 'Come and eat this lot, or we will have to throw it out.' We went over to the table, but Ralph was still not too happy about it. He looks at the big plate of food.

'You shouldn't have . . .'

'Eat it up,' the teacher says, and started into his lot, not looking up any more. The boy tried eating with his knife and fork, but he just kept pushing things off the plate. The teacher's wife looked as if she wasn't paying any attention –

but she was. She came over and put her hand on the boy's shoulder.

'Eat it with your fingers, love,' she says. The teacher looked up. 'Don't pay attention to us civilized beings son,' he says. The boy must have understood, because he started into it with his hands.

'What about yourself?' Ralph says to Mrs Burney.

'Oh, I'm all right,' she says. 'I have had something already.'

'Are you sure?' he says.

'What if Ma and Da and them all come up,' I say.

'They'll not take him,' Ralph says.

'I know that,' I say. 'But you're not his Da.' There was egg running down the boy's chin and he was trying to push it back up into his mouth with his fingers.

'He's not his Da,' I say to the teacher. 'So maybe they have got a right to him, more than Ralph.' The teacher didn't seem to be too worried about it.

'We will cross that bridge when we come to it,' he says.

'You're not going to bring anything up, are you?' the teacher's wife says.

Ralph looked a bit bewildered, like he sometimes did when he couldn't follow the conversation. But he didn't say nothing and the teacher just said to his wife, 'Don't worry, dear, I won't bring anything up unless I have to.'

We finished eating and went out to the teacher's old van. The dog came too. It and Ralph and the boy sat in the back seat and I sat in the front beside the teacher.

The van started all right, but it was terribly noisy although there was cardboard stuck in at the sides of the windows to keep them from vibrating. We tried to shout at each other for a while. Then we gave up and just sat and watched the road running into the nose of the van. It was a fair distance to the town. Further than I had ever gone before. We had to go through the village where our new house was but we didn't have to pass by the side of the housing estate, although we could see the mass of red tiled roofs from the main street. Nobody said anything about it.

Soon the houses got closer and closer together – until they were crammed on top of each other and we were in the town. You could smell it – new things and fish and chips and hair oil. I said that I wanted fish and chips, but Ralph said to shut up. There was a car nosing out in front of us, but it stopped and waved us on. The teacher waved and we all waved too, and went on ahead. Ralph said that many another chap would have driven straight out. When we were up near the end of another street a policeman nodded for us to stop, and he came over, and we all said, 'Hallo'.

'Did you not see the sign at the bottom?' he says to the teacher.

'No,' the teacher says. 'I didn't. If you were to read all the signs in here you wouldn't have time to see where you are going.' The van eased forward and shuddered and conked out.

'It's a one-way street,' the policeman shouts.

'It wasn't last time I was in this town.'

'Well it is now,' the policeman says. 'You'd better go back.'

'We are almost at the end now,' the teacher says and pulls the starter.

'Look, I don't make the rules here. I'm only here to see that they're carried out.'

'All right.' The teacher laughs. 'We will go back.'

The policeman came over apologetically. 'Whoever designed this town didn't design it for traffic,' he says.

'No,' the teacher says. 'And whoever designed this country, didn't design it for towns.' The policeman didn't know whether the teacher was being funny or not, but he gave us a half smile all the same, and we reversed back.

'It wasn't a one way street last time I was here either,' Ralph says.

'They speak different in here,' I say.

When we got outside the optician's there was room for us to park. There was a great big pair of glasses in the window, made out of electric light.

'Do you want a pair like that son?' The teacher pointed and we all laughed. He took the boy by the hand and went in. The dog wouldn't keep quiet no matter what Ralph said to it – it whimpered like a baby. They were in a long time and Ralph and me wondered if we should toot the horn to tell them to hurry up. There was a lot of people went past. One man came out of the dentist's beside the optician's: he was spitting blood on the footpath, and his handkerchief was red with blood too. A drunk man staggered against the window of the van and asked me for twopence, for a cup of the tea.

'I got nothing,' I say. Then Ralph reaches over and gives him a threepence piece.

'God bless you,' he says and staggers away. He looked like the world was turning around and he had to keep moving his feet to stay in the same place or maybe go on a bit.

When the boy came out you wouldn't have noticed him, only his mouth was still hanging open. He had on a pair of dark-rimmed glasses, and the glass thinner too, and he looked like he could see better or he had got more sense. The teacher said that they were only a temporary measure – that the ones he had been wearing had been wrong ones and they might have done his eyes harm. The optician said that he wanted the boy to wear these ones for about a month, then he would have to go back for another test.

'That's all right,' Ralph says. 'We'll bring him in.'

'Show him your appointment card, Herby,' the teacher says. The boy put his hand into his blazer pocket and brought out the pink card. Ralph was so pleased he put his arm around him and pressed him tight. For the first time I seen the boy giving a real smile.

'Now,' the teacher says, 'I am going to get him lots of cards like that, and he is going to learn the different colours.' The teacher was pleased too.

'That's pink, son,' Ralph says, and the boy smiled again.

'We can get lots of cards and he can put the different colours together,' the teacher says.

'And he can get ones to match my paints,' Ralph says.

'Maybe you can get him on to painting a tree,' I say.

'It will all come slowly,' the teacher says.

We went into a red café where the girls wore pink overalls. We had fish and chips and the boy had an extra piece of fish, because Ralph said it was good for your brains. There was jiggy music on and Ralph tapped time on the red table. The table was covered with a sheet of glass and someone had slid a piece of paper under it that said:

'It's only nature after all;
To take a little girl behind the wall.
To pull down her protections,
And stick in your connexion.
It's only nature after all.
Signed:

SHAKESPEARE'

'It's okay,' I say, 'if they don't come and take him away to a home or something.'

'I'll not let them – not now,' Ralph says.

'I reckon we can learn him more,' I say. 'But we're not his Da and Ma.'

'We will cross that bridge when we come to it,' the teacher says.

'You would think by you, you're not worried,' I say.

'Say no more about it now,' he says. And even Ralph looks at him in an odd way.

The teacher pays and we go out and further down the street to a pub. Everybody there knows the teacher – they call him the Master. We sit round the table with three old men. One of the men got up and asked us what we were for. Ralph and the teacher said they would have a Guinness and me and the boy had lemonade.

'Here's one for you,' the little man with the wheeze in his throat says, and we all went silent. He was dead serious.

'What goes round and round in the water and never touches it?' he says.

'I don't know,' Ralph says.

'There's the smart one there,' the old man says pointing to the teacher. The other two men sat calmly smoking their pipes, but looking as if they had been listening to the old man's riddles for twenty years.

'No, Johnnie, you have got me there,' the teacher confessed.

'Man, oh man,' the old man says. 'And you a schoolteacher.'

'Tell us,' we all say. We all had to look as if we were trying to rack our brains trying to find the answer and we all had to ask him for a long time before he told us.

'An egg in a duck's arse,' he says. We all made noises like we should have got it – as if we should have thought of a simple thing like that.

'Why the hell didn't I think of that,' the teacher says. The old man got more excited now and his breathing got worse, but it didn't seem to worry him all that much.

'What's rid from the inside and blew all over?' he says.

'A pot of paint,' Ralph says.

'No,' the old man wheezes. 'How do you make that out?'

'I know,' the teacher says.

'Right tell me.'

'A fart,' he says.

'You guessed it,' the old man said, and laughed a rough thick laugh, and took a glut of Guinness to wash the thick snot from his throat.

'You see rid from the inside – not red and blue all over,' he explained.

It was late when we left the pub, but the chat was good. One old man told us how when he was young, you could get a drink on a Sunday – that is if you were a bona fide traveller – that meant that you had to travel more than three miles from where you lived. If you got caught in a pub nearer than that, you would get fined.

'These old blokes know their stuff,' Ralph says and the teacher agreed. We were all a bit plastered. And I hardly knew the time going in because we sang most of the way.

'Maybe I better call and let Ma know I'm all right,' I say when we come to the village.

'All right,' the teacher says. 'But we will wait outside in the van for you.'

There was just Derek in. He was lying upside down on an armchair, humming a hymn through a comb and a piece of tissue paper. The knob on the TV set was turned down, so that the man's face was flattened.

'Where is everybody?' I asked. He swung his feet off the wall and toppled onto the floor.

'They're all in hospital,' he says and gets up and sits on the chair looking serious. 'You know that advert on the TV that says, Drink a pint of milk a day. Well Da got that into his head and all he would say was, Drink a pint of milk a day, Drink a pint of milk a day, no matter what anybody said to him. And he left a note for the milkman saying, Leave a hundred pints of milk. The milkman went and told the doctor and the doctor said he would have to go.'

'Stop that fool talk,' I say. 'Where are they?'

'Gone to heaven,' he says. 'There was a big chair of fire

came down the morning and they went out and got into it. The last I seen they were heading towards heaven – whether they got in or not, I'm not sure. It's true,' he says. 'All the neighbours were down to see them go.' Then Wendy came down dressed like a film star.

'Where's Ma and Da?' I say.

'Away up to the old house a whole load of them,' she says.

'Who?' I say.

'Ma and Da and Andy and the Reverend Marks and Aunt Mary.'

'What for?'

'To get the boy,' she says. She takes out a little gold bottle from her handbag and dabs a bit on her tongue.

'What's that for?' I say.

'Gold Spot,' she says. 'It's to make your breath smell nice when you're kissing.'

'What do they want the boy for?'

'They got to get him and take him to the doctor, and when the doctor certifies him dim-witted and gives them a letter, then they can put him in an institution,' she says.

'He's okay with Ralph,' I say.

'I am taking nothing more to do with this house,' she says in a polite voice. 'My boy friend and I are going on our honeymoon soon. So we have other things to think about. Adios,' she says and went out.

'What's going on?' I say.

'She's running away to get married,' Derek says.

'Well I better go,' I say. 'The teacher is waiting for me in the van.'

'I'll come to,' he says. 'There's nothing happening down here no more.'

Derek came with us, and he was surprised to see the boy looking so well. He told us that it was really true – that they had all gone to get the boy to put him in an institution.

Ralph says that they couldn't do that if the boy didn't want to go. But Derek says, once a doctor writes a letter to say you are mad, there's not a thing you can do about it – once they get you on paper.

'That seems to be the way things are going these days,' the teacher agrees. 'But we will see what we can do about it.'

We went straight to the teacher's place, and Andy's car was parked close to the door.

'They're here,' the teacher says.

'They can't do this,' Ralph says and looks at the boy – like he was thinking: if they do this, he might as well be dead. We pulled up close to Andy's car. He had Christ dangling from a piece of elastic at the back window.

'How did they all get in there?' I say.

'Things will be all right, Ralph,' the teacher says in a soft voice.

For the first time I noticed softness in Derek's voice. 'I'm behind you in this, Ralph,' he says. 'I know you're doing the boy good.' Then as if he noticed the tenderness in his own voice, and didn't like it, he says, 'dim-witted eejit as he is.'

The dog was sleeping with its head on the boy's lap, and it put its head up slow when the teacher stopped the van.

Mrs Burney met us at the door, and she whispered that they were all in there, waiting for us in the living-room.

'You take the boy and keep him in the kitchen for a while,' the teacher says to his wife. 'And we will see how things go.' The boy took Mrs Burney's hand and went into the kitchen with her. He was looking really well now. The teacher looked round at Ralph.

'Don't worry, Ralph,' he says. 'My wife will see that he comes to no harm.'

'It's okay,' Ralph says, trying to laugh, but inside you could tell his guts were tightening up with fear.

It was a big living-room, smelling of flowers. They were all there. Da was saying that if people thought about others instead of thinking about themselves, the world would be a far nicer place to live in. Ma said that Da should go into Parliament with a mind like his. Da said that he was only stating a fact.

Aunt Mary was sitting in the corner beside Andy. She had no children hanging on her. She was wearing a brown coat with new buttons sewn on it – with royal blue cotton. Andy was wearing his usual overcoat, and you could tell by the big square bulges in it that his pockets were full of Bibles.

The Reverend Marks came over and gave the teacher's hand a good hard shake. The teacher just said, 'Sit down.' And the Reverend Marks went back and sat where he had been sitting. His collar was round and shiny and it looked like it would be on him for ever. He looked very new.

Ralph took a couple of quick steps into the room and blushed, and stopped and touched his nose with his hand. Then put his hands down straight and walked stiffly to a seat. He sank low in it, then pulled himself up onto the edge and concentrated hard on one of the teacher's pictures, not looking at anyone.

The teacher waited until Derek and me were seated. Then he took a seat by the door and crossed his legs easily and let his hands rest on his lap. 'Well,' he says, 'it looks like a prayer meeting.' Andy was sniffing and grinning – nobody spoke.

'I said it looks like a prayer meeting,' he says again, only this time he was looking directly at the Reverend Marks. The Reverend Marks shone with cleanness, and he giggled.

There is one question I would like to put to you,' he says to Ralph, 'Where is the boy?'

'In another room – he . . .' Ralph says.

'I see.'

'He's all right where he is,' Ralph says quick.

'So you are the only one who knows where he is – you are the one in control,' the Reverend Marks says.

'No,' Ralph says. He was sweating now and I felt sorrier for him than I had ever felt. I could have killed the Reverend Marks, but the teacher's eyes were watching the whole thing, and I stayed still.

'We will leave the boy where he is at the moment,' the Reverend Marks said. 'But don't you think the boy would be better with his own mother who is arranging for him to have special treatment.' He was looking round at everybody, but talking to Ralph. He put his hand out. 'These good people have all got a good interest in the boy – they have all got the boy at heart.' Ma nodded and Andy grinned – he grinned all the time, but he grinned worse when the Reverend Marks looked at him. 'In this world we should all work for the good of one another.' Da nodded. And the Reverend Marks saw him and went on: 'I am not saying you are bad for the boy, but, I stress, but, you can never replace the mother's love for the child.'

'Cluck-cluck,' the teacher says, but the Reverend Marks goes on.

'You will agree that two heads are better than one. We have got together – your mother and your father, and of course Andy here has been a great help, and of course your Aunt Mary and myself.'

'It's not the first time,' Derek sniggers.

Andy swung his body back and forth and his face got red. 'It is Jasus working in us,' he says. 'Jasus died for sinners – we are all sinners.'

'Eejit,' Derek says loud. Ma tightens her lips at him and he tightens his back at her.

'I don't care who died for who,' Ralph says. 'But the boy's happy here with me.'

'He has always been like that,' Da says. 'He won't see the other point of view.'

'Do you see his point of view?' the teacher says.

'Yes,' Da says. 'Yes, sir, we have looked into the matter and legally Ralph has no right to the boy – he had no right to take him.'

'You stay out of this,' Aunt Mary says. 'You stay out of this – a balmy teacher.'

'Do you really think so? Then you have a short memory,' the teacher says. He goes out and comes in with the boy by the hand. He leaves him in the middle of the floor. The boy looks around a bit, then he goes straight to Ralph and tries to squeeze himself onto the chair beside him.

'Does that mean anything to you?' the teacher says. 'The love between Ralph and the boy.' Ralph rests his hand on the boy's shoulder and the boy leans back against him. Aunt Mary reaches for the boy, and pulls him towards her. The boy holds onto Ralph, but she gives him a good hard tug that nearly makes the boy fall onto her knees.

'Stay here, stay away from the filthy brock. If you would get yourself a girl friend it would answer you better,' she says to Ralph.

Ralph's eyes are glassy. 'What do you mean?' he says, 'I like him, like he likes me.'

'Shut your mouth,' Aunt Mary says.

'You have no right to him by law,' Da says.

'He'll not listen to you,' Ma says.

The Reverend Marks stood up. 'It is right what your father says. You have no right to him by the laws of God nor the laws of man.'

Ralph's mouth was twitching at the sides, and I kept saying to myself, 'Don't cry Ralph, don't let them see you cry.' He looked at the teacher and the teacher winked and Ralph looked away, not knowing where to look.

'We understand how you feel,' the Reverend Marks says.

'But we will have to take the boy away for his own good.'
Ma and Da stood up, and the boy was looking lost in the
middle of the floor.

Suddenly the teacher stood up and went loud: 'Cock-a-
doodle-do.' Then he says, 'Sit down – all of you on your
arses, before I knock you down.' They all sat down. Ma
nearly sat on Da's knee. Her face was red – all their faces
were red and the Reverend Marks ran his finger round the
inside of his collar now, as if it was too tight – but it
wasn't.

'We better go on home now,' Aunt Mary says. The boy
had gone back to Ralph. Andy was looking a bit mystified,
but he was still grinning.

'Have you got a short memory, Mary?' the teacher says.

'Let me go home,' she says – and not bothering with the
boy now. Her face is red and it is hard to tell whether she
is embarrassed or angry.

'Sit down,' the teacher says in a very firm voice, and
his eyes are staring like a madman's – like I have never seen
before. 'I have got to remind you all again – and you know if
you try to take this boy away, I will disgrace you all.' He
looks at the Reverend Marks. 'Yes, you are in this too – the
boy is your child.'

'Nobody's to say nothing if they haven't facts to go on,'
Da says.

'Oh, but I have,' the teacher says. 'This boy was a disgrace
to Mary and the Reverend Marks here – if he can be called
that. This woman,' the teacher says, looking at Aunt Mary,
who was tightening her fists, and shaking too. She tries to
get up and the teacher pushes her down again. 'Yes you,'
he says. 'You put this boy – this baby – in a hen house, you
cunt. You almost killed him.' He looks at the Reverend
Marks. 'Yes, and you knew all the time, yet you smiled and
gave your lousy sermons – you wanted the child to be dead
more than anything – you didn't even want him to be seen,

even after you knew that I had found out.' Ma was sticking her nails into her face. 'Yes and you,' the teacher says to her. 'You knew all the time. Why do you think the Reverend Marks here had to get you a new house? Not because Ralph was ill, but because he was frightened in case you would squeal on him. Can you imagine what this child suffered – can you imagine what he was like when I found him? You have made him sick enough, you bastards – now get out of my house before I throw you out. And do good elsewhere.'

They were going – they were already halfway out the door. Da was the last one out.

'I never knew nothing about this,' he says. 'And you were right to speak your mind.'

When the master closed the door, I could imagine them all jogging away in Andy's little car, with Christ dangling from a piece of elastic at the back window.

The boy was sitting between Ralph's legs and he was telling him to go and show Derek his appointment card. Derek says, 'Come over, I'll not eat you.'